# The Glitches

*The Glitch*

*The Empties*

*The Norm*

RELAY PUBLISHING EDITION, APRIL 2017

Copyright © 2017 Relay Publishing Ltd.

*Cover Art by Rebecca Frank Art*

www.relaypub.com

# THE NORM

The Glitches Series

Book Three

**Ramona Finn**

# Blurb

Can a Glitch ever overcome her programming?

Escaping the AI's clutches came with a heavy price, but Lib is about the find out the worst is yet to come. While Lib is desperately searching for answers in her mother's former home, the abandoned Empties, an earthquake engineered by the AI drives her and her friends underground, forcing them to decide their course of action once and for all: keep hiding forever or face the AI head on. Lib knows remaining hidden means certain death, but convincing the Rogues to follow her may be an impossible task.

As the group takes shelter in a secret underground facility, Lib unwittingly discovers the birthplace of the AI. She hatches a plan to turn the system against itself, but it means asking Wolf and the Rogues to do the one thing they never would. Lib's connection with Wolf feels unbreakable, but her plan will force him to sacrifice everything he's ever known.

Breaking into the Norm is the easy part—now, Lib must face an enemy far worse than she could've anticipated. If she fails to overcome her programming and defeat the AI, it means the friends she's come to see as family will never survive.

**Sign up to Ramona Finn's mailing list to be notified of new releases and get exclusive excerpts!**

Sign Up at

www.ramonafinn.com

You can also find me on Facebook!

www.facebook.com/ramonafinnbooks

# Table of Contents

# Chapter One

"There hasn't been a lot of activity from the Norm—do you think the AI is dead?" Skye glances at me from the broken window where she stands, facing the horizon. "Do you think...think Raj is dead?"

I can only shake my head. I just don't know. In a way it's funny...the more I learn the less I seem to know about anything.

We've come to the Empties looking for... something. I am still drawn to the Empties, to the deserted buildings of what was once a city. If I squint, I can almost see it as it must have once been with gleaming towers of metal and glass and wide paved paths and trees and people. Now it is dust and twisted chunks of metal and only a few places that still hold secrets—as this building might with its only half broken windows and bits of metal and furnishings.

Most of the buildings in the Empties are towering monoliths, aged and broken with few reminders of what they once held. Every now and then we find useful metal, or paper—I can read most of it, although I don't know why. I have no memories of learning—but, then, the AI created me. I am not a Rogue—someone born outside the Norm. I am not a Glitch—a Tech from the Norm that went wrong. I am something else. And I am still coming to terms with that.

And was Conie—the AI—right? Am I the key to the survival of the human race?

Glancing around, I wonder why people left the Empties in a hurry. I think something happened—a flood along with other disasters. I have…not my memories but those of Dr. Constance Sig who created the AI. And then the AI created me, using some of Dr. Sig and something artificial. But I am more than that. Dr. Sig's memories sometimes show up now and then as dreams, but I know how I am seeing what she once saw. Somehow the AI gave me some of those memories—but I wish I had more.

I know everyone fled to the domes built by Dr. Sig. But now only one domed area is left – the Norm – controlled by the AI. Is she dead? Did Raj's virus damage her? Or only slow her down? His code wasn't complete, so I don't think it will stop the AI.

Standing up from the pile of scrap I have collected, I stretch my back and tell Skye, "Conie could be just repairing herself. I don't think Raj's virus took her down."

*Conie*—I still give the AI a name. She is more like a person to me—she wears the face of Dr. Constance Sig, but she is my enemy. She once sent me out of the Norm to find the Glitches—to find the Rogues who lived with Glitches—so she could destroy them. When I failed her, she tried to kill me. But now she seems to think I am something special. I have become more than I was meant to be. And I want to use that if I can.

I don't really know what I am—am I part human and part something else? Lifting my hand I stare at it. I can be hurt. I can bleed. But do I have biogear inside me? Am I really more like Conie than I want to be?

Skye moves and I look up at her. She walks back to my side and gives a tired smile, but it seems to me she seems almost relieved. She has always wanted to go back to the Norm, so of course she would not want to hear it is gone forever. She glances around us. "Sun's coming up. We should head back to the tunnels."

I nod. Daylight is not as dangerous as it once was—we have not seen drones or scabs from the Norm in days now. But I keep remembering how Conie said she would have the Norm ready to leave this world in four solar months. I don't know how much time that is, but I keep feeling it is not long. And something keeps pulling me back to the Empties. Why do I feel as if the answer to stopping the AI is here? Is this another memory from Dr. Sig? Maybe it's a memory the AI didn't know I got from Dr. Sig?

We have gone higher than any other Rogue—or Glitch—has ever gone in the Empties, climbing up wobbling stairs and using ropes to pull us higher in the tallest building. Even so, the Norm is only a black lump on the horizon—a curve of dark dome.

The AI has not been sending drones or scabs to work on the dome, to make it ready for space. Is that because the work is done—or because Raj was able to help us and slow her down? I hope that Conie is still holding Raj, but I don't know if that's true.

There are too many questions. But one thing we do know—most of the platforms we once used to hack the Norm for water and other supplies are dead. That isn't good. And it's another

3

reason to explore the Empties. We can scavenge some food from the plants and animals we hunt—but where are we going to get more water?

I don't have an answer to that. Yet.

After putting the scrap into my pouch, I follow Skye. The pouch bounces against my hip as I head down from the building after her. We leave the rope we used to get here in place—we may come back.

We pass through a few rooms on the way down to the wobbly stairs.

Up this high, we found a few chunks of metal the Rogues can use. Most of the ground level has been scavenged by the Rogues for as long as anyone remembers. We also found gear, but most of it is badly damaged. I no longer wear my biogear, but sometimes my skin itches for the connection and I think about making a new set. The biogear made me stronger, faster and I miss those abilities. But I fear now that it was making me too much like the AI. If I already have biogear inside me, I don't need more gear turning me into another AI.

Part of me fears that's what Raj may be now.

It wasn't Raj that I saw the last time I was in the Norm—it was a program with Raj's face. But I hang onto the hope that Raj is alive somewhere—maybe in stasis. Maybe because the AI fears his virus may work and so she sees a need for him.

My heart clenches and I rub at my chest. I promised to go back for Raj and I did—but I did not save him. How am I supposed to save everyone if I cannot even save a friend?

Heading across another room, I glance out dirty windows. Streaks of orange light flitter across the room, making me squint. The sun is coming up.

Reaching the ground again, we head for where we left the AT. It's Rogue tradition to leave the four-wheel vehicles outside the Empties. I don't know why. It would be faster to travel through the wide paved paths on an AT. On the other hand, going on foot means that every now and then you find something that was overlooked. I like it best when I find things I can read that tell me about the past—there are so few of those around.

Glancing around, for an instant I see the Empties as Dr. Sig must have once—bright and strong. The images flash and vanish and I stare again at twisted metal and dust and crumbling walls.

Wetness leaks from my eyes and I wipe at my cheeks.

Glancing back at me, Skye shifts the pouch on her shoulder and asks, "Do you think Mech…I mean the Rejects, do you think they're okay?"

I shake my head. "If they can hide from the AI, they'll be okay."

Skye flips the bright tail of her hair over her shoulder. "We should go see them again. Didn't you say we would? They'll know if the AI is still active or damaged."

I don't want to go near the Norm—not right now. But Skye is right.

We reach the AT and Skye climbs into the driver's seat. I swing a leg up and over behind her. I glance at the Empties, certain I am leaving something important behind. What did I miss?

Suddenly the metal towers sway, and the AT jumps underneath us as if Skye had started it, but I don't hear a whine—I only hear a low rumbling and then crashes from the Empties. Looking at it, it's as if everything is moving and shaking

Skye turns to me, her eyes huge. "What is it?"

The rumbling lasts only a few moments, and then stops. Glancing around, I see dust in the air. "It's like the ground...moved."

Standing up on the back of the AT, I stare at where I know the Norm is—it seems taller. I can see the top of the Norm now whereas before I couldn't have seen it from this height. And suddenly I know what it was—the AI. She is testing to see if the Norm can be pulled away from this world. She is still with us—and she is going to destroy this world in order to protect the false world she runs.

Wetting her lips, Skye says, "We should get back to the new tunnels."

I can only nod, but hear metal shrieking. I glance back at the Empties. One of the twisted metal towers that was leaning is slowly falling—and heading straight at us. I yell at Skye, "Go! Now."

She gets the AT started. It hums to life. I stare at the huge structure falling toward us. All I hear is the tearing scream of metal, a shrill sound. The AT jerks forward, and Skye heads into the vast space of the Outside. But the building is still falling. Tapping on Skye's shoulder, I wave for her to turn, curve away from the falling tower. It creaks, groans and slams into the ground behind us, sending a cloud of dirt into the air, leaving us choking.

Skye slows the AT so we can glance back. "Lot of metal we can scavenge now."

There is. Twisted, smashed chunks of metal darken the land around the Empties. I cough. It seems to me the ground is still shaking—and then I remember one of my dreams about the tunnels where the Rogues live falling down. Would shaking earth do that?

Turning to Skye, I tell her, "We have to get back to the new tunnels—now." But what I am really thinking is I have to get back to Wolf.

# Chapter Two

The wind whips away the hum of the AT. Skye pushes it faster than is really safe—I don't know if she's as worried as I am or if my worry is pushing her. The AT jumps over the ground, wheels shaking up dust.

The Tracker Clan moved already to new tunnels. We're supposed to leave the ATs hidden and away from the tunnels, but I urge Skye to head to one of the entrances. She shakes her head and takes us up onto a ridge overlooking the new tunnels.

For a moment I see only dust.

Survival means hiding, living beneath the surface in natural tunnels that sprawl beneath the hills, using underground hot springs if we can, and staying out of the overbearing sun—and away from the AI's drones.

Shading my eyes against the rising sun, which already burns my skin, I glance around. The bad part about tunnels is that they can collapse. Are the new tunnels strong enough to have survived the ground shaking like it did in the Empties?

Everything seems still, and then dusty figures emerge from the ground.

Sand sifts off them, sliding off hair and skin and the leathers the Rogues wear. In front of me Skye lets out a breath and starts counting. I know what she's doing—we have only twenty-six left in the Tracker Clan. We should see twenty-four come out of the tunnels. They stagger out and it is impossible to tell who is

8

who—but I know Wolf is taller and bigger than any other Rogue. They're all moving slow, coughing as if they swallowed dirt—or as if the dirt almost swallowed them.

My chest tightens. I squint to try and see better and wish I had biogear on.

Skye nudges the AT's nose to one side. "We should go. Park this and help them."

I nod. It seems to take too long to hide the AT. I want this done. I want to find Wolf. Skye's hands are shaking, but she makes sure the AT is hidden under a dirt-colored cloth so if drones do fly overhead they won't see it. I almost snap at her and tell her it doesn't matter, but it does. We can't risk losing the new tunnels—they are the last set of tunnels we have in this area. Biting on the side of my cheek, heart hammering, I try to remember we have to do what is right for the clan.

At last the AT is covered. Skye breaks into a jog, I run past her. I'm sweating and breathing hard and the sun beats down on my shoulders when I reach the others. Almost everyone is sitting in the shade of the rocks, trying to find some cover from the sun. I look for the faces I know best—Wolf, Crow, Bird, Dat, Alis, Pike, Croc. Trouble is I know every face in the Tracker Clan. But no one looks right with dirt streaking their faces.

No one speaks, but a few moan as if they're hurt. Soft sobs reach my ears.

Shaking limbs, I glance around again. Where is Wolf?

Every face the wrong one. Too lean, too narrow, too round or square. Panic swells in my chest in a hard knot.

*What if he didn't get—?*

I won't let myself finish the thought. Wolf has to be fine. Has to be. Wolf is leader of the Tracker Clan. Wolf…Wolf saved me. He can't be… but the knots inside tighten. I've lost Raj. I've lost others. Chandra and Marc. Lizard and Sidewinder. And so many others—most of them because of the AI. Nothing in this world *has* to be fine.

At last I see Crow's tall, lanky form. He shakes the dirt from his hair, brushes it off the scar on his face. His shirt is torn and more dirt clings to the stubble on his. He seems made of dirt, but his gold and green eyes spark with anger.

I let out a breath, call his name and head over to him. "What happened?"

He reaches for me and pulls me against his chest. "You got out. You and Skye?" Good." He hugs me tightly, but I pull back.

He seems reluctant but lets me slide from his arms. "When the shaking started, we didn't think it'd be this bad." He runs a hand through his thick hair. It's dirty and disheveled. "Bird got the warning out. Said to run, get to the Outside."

"Wolf?" The word slips out. Glancing around, I still don't see him.

Crow shakes his head. "Don't know. He'd be last out."

My chest tightens. I clear my throat and slap Crow's shoulder, sending up a cloud of dust. "You made it. That's good. I have to find Wolf."

Crow frowns and rubs the scar on his cheek. "I need to help Croc."

He moves away, heading to where Croc is bending over a woman who is stretched out on the ground, moaning. I don't know who it is, but I think it might be one of the council members—Elk maybe. I know it's not Bird because there are no fluttering ribbons in this woman's hair or on her clothing. Croc stands out because he's older than almost everyone else, and sun glints off the skin on his head. The wind tugs at his dark, thinning hair. I have never seen him look so tired—or so worried. He moves from the woman to another Rogue, someone almost unrecognizable due to the dirt caked on the small body. But I think it must be Mouse. She's cradling her arm, but at least she is sitting upright.

Worrying at my lip with my teeth, I start to count how many made it out of the tunnels. I come up with sixteen, including me and Skye. Turning, I walk to the edge of the dark hole. It seems too small now—smaller than it was when Skye and I left last night. There are other exits—the Tracker Clan always has backup exits. Maybe the others got out there. Edging closer, I glance down, and I worry that if I get close maybe I'll make it cave in. I don't trust the ground anymore.

Leaning over the hole, I call out, "Wolf?"

A hand settles on my shoulder. My heart jumps, but I turn and see only Skye. "He might have gotten out at one of the other exits."

Swallowing hard, I nod. "I haven't seen Bird either. Crow said she gave the warning."

Skye glances around and then wraps her arms tight around her middle. "What happened? Why'd the ground shake like that?"

I don't want to get into that now—I don't want to tell her what I suspect. What I know must be true. I want to find Wolf.

After a moment, I just say, my voice flat, "I need to find Wolf."

Turning from Skye, I head to check the other exits. I find two of them gone. There are just dips in the ground where there used to be holes that led down into the tunnels. My stomach twists as if I'm going to be sick. I keep thinking about Wolf—about his rare smile, about his strong, wide hands. About how he taught me to defend myself, how he made me part of the Tracker Clan. I think about Bird, too. We've had our disagreements, but what would the clan do without Bird and her odd visions?

At the third tunnel exit, I find Alis sitting on a rock, holding her sides as if she's hurt. She's hunched over, her shoulders shaking. Dirt streaks her pale face and coats her hair until you can hardly tell the color is red. Her braid looks more like a halo of loose ends.

I move to her, kneel and put a hand on her shoulder. "Alis, are you hurt?"

She looks up, eyes rimmed red. She opens her mouth, but no words come out. She coughs and spits out mud. I pat her thin arms and legs, searching for cuts or broken bones. She stares blankly, her green eyes dull. Alis is a Glitch, much like I was, but she's always been chatty and it unnerves me to see her like this—she looks broken inside.

Taking her shoulders, I turn her so she has to face me. "What's wrong?" Her lower lip trembles. Wetness slides from her eyes, mixing with the dirt on her face to leave ugly streaks. I want to shake her, but I worry she is really hurt. "We need to get you to Croc."

I stand and pull her to her feet. She glances down at the tunnel hole and then looks at me. "Dat." She wets her lips. "Dat went back to get some of the biogear. He said we couldn't leave all that gear behind. He went back. I yelled at him, but he went back. And the…the rocks just fell down."

I glance down into the tunnel. Dat is down there—and I don't know if he's dead or trapped or hurt. "Wait here," I tell Alis. I head for the tunnel hole, but Alis grabs my arms.

Her fingers dig into my flesh, and when I look at her she is shaking her head, her eyes wild. "No. No use. I tried."

Glancing down at her fingers, I see they're bloody. She must have tried to dig Dat out. I shudder.

Alis slaps a hand over her mouth, but a sob escapes. She meets my gaze and tells me, her voice shaking, "You can't go back. The rocks—the tunnel's gone."

"Maybe he got out another way. Dat's small…and smart."

Alis shakes her head. "He was just a Glitch. The Rogues won't care that he was just a Glitch."

Grabbing her arms, I shake her. "No one is just anything. I will check the other tunnels. You go find Croc. Follow my steps here. Get to the others." I pull away from Alis and take a step back, waiting to see if she's going to do what I've told her to do.

She stares at me a moment, then nods. Turning away, she staggers back, following my trail. I glance down at the tunnel hole. When Alis is gone, I slip down inside, using the ropes we always have set up to get in and out. But Alis is right—there is no going anywhere in any tunnel from here. I land on the dirt and around me I see only boulders and rocks. Sand trickles down from the top of what was once a tunnel and now is only a wall of jagged rocks—that's what Alis bloodied her hands clawing at.

"Dat, you get out—you find another way out," I mutter. But I know that even with biogear, no one can claw through that much rock. Climbing back out again, I sit for a moment on the ground, pulling in deep breaths. The sun is hot, but inside I am chilled. Now I fear for Dat.

Standing, I try to shake away the cold.

*Find Wolf. Just find Wolf.*

Wolf always knows what to do. Wolf…I have to admit now that I care for Wolf more than I probably should. I've been a Glitch…an outsider to the clan. I came from the Norm. I am something…different. Wolf is a born Rogue—this is his clan, his place. And he can't be gone.

Starting out again, I check the rest of the tunnels. Two more are gone—they're not even dips in the ground, but I see the lines where tunnels once were and now I see only jagged lines across the ground. The longer it takes to find him, the more my chest hurts. The more the idea I *won't* find him buzzes inside my head like angry insects.

Wolf has to be—the clan needs him. And I do, too.

I have one tunnel exit left—one that I know about, at least. Maybe there are more, but this is the last one I was shown when we moved to the new tunnels after our last battle with the AI. I have to climb down into a canyon. Rocks skin my palms. I'm sweating. My skin shirt sticks to my back and my boots slip on the boulders. Once at the bottom, I turn the corner and for a moment I fear no one is here—and then someone moves.

Wolf crouches over the tunnel exit, pulling Bird out. She's coughing. Dirt coats both of them, making them blend into the sand. Wolf pulls Bird to the ground and shakes the dust from his thick, long hair. His dark skin is left pale by the dirt. If I could see his eyes right now, I know they would be darker than the night.

"Wolf!" I shout, already running to him.

At the sound of my voice, he turns to me. I reach him and throw my arms around him. For an instant, he holds me. For five pounding heart beats it is only Wolf holding me that matters. And then I hear Bird coughing. Pulling back, I drop my arms to my sides.

Bird looks dazed. A jagged cut across her forehead is bleeding, mixing with the dirt to leave a black streak running down the side of her face.

She staggers a step and I reach out to steady her, but she slaps my hand away. "I'm alright."

Wolf gives a snort and scoops Bird up into his arms. She glares at him, and I tell myself not to be jealous of Bird—she needs the help. Turning to Wolf, I see he has a bruise swelling on his cheek. Blood and dust coat his bare arms. "You sure you're up to carrying her?"

Wolf gives me a flat look and asks, "Where've you been?"

"Doesn't matter. We should get Bird to Croc." Turning, I lead the way back to the others. We take the long way, winding through the canyon and then crossing over a ridgeline and coming back down to what was once the main tunnel entrance.

When Wolf has Bird settled with Croc, he turns to me. "Did everyone get out?"

I shrug. "Haven't counted." And I haven't…but I have been looking for Dat. For his curling mop of hair and his pale, dirt-covered skin and his slim, short body. I haven't seen him. I glance around now, and do a quick count. With Wolf and Bird here, that makes it eighteen out, including Skye and me. That means eight are missing still.

I take a breath and let it out, then face Wolf.

Wolf is staring at me, his dark eyes as unreadable as ever. But just having him here—strong, big, solid—makes me feel better. "I'm worried about Dat."

Wolf nods. "We need to check all the exits." He moves away before I can tell him I've done that. Maybe Wolf will find something I didn't—maybe he knows about an exit I don't know about.

Soon, Wolf heads out with three others who aren't hurt—Pike, Crow and Skye go with him. I can't face those tunnels—or the fear that we have lost eight of the clan. Heading over to Croc, I ask if he needs help. He flashes me a tight smile, shoves water and a rag at me and tells me, "Clean up the minor cuts. Get me if anything doesn't look so minor."

I spent most of the day helping Croc. We have only one who is badly hurt—Elk. A rock fell on her and Croc tells me he doesn't think she will last the night. He gives her herbs to help her sleep and ease her pain. Two others have broken bones—an arm and a hand. Croc binds the wounds, but he keeps looking into the pouch hanging from his shoulder and muttering, "I don't have enough."

Looking around, I realize we have so very little—our food stores are down in the tunnels. Our water stores are there, too. We have a few supplies on the ATs, but not enough to last more than a few days. Night is also coming and the Outside will go from too hot to cold. Most everyone here has only what they were wearing—meaning no coats. We're in more trouble than I thought.

17

When Wolf comes back, his mouth is set tight. He comes back with only those who went out with him. I close my eyes and vow I will remember Dat—I will remember his face, his name, how he was almost as smart as Raj. My throat tightens and my eyes sting, but Wolf's voice pulls me back to the moment.

"We need a scavenge for water—we can cut some plants, maybe risk a fire. But we can't stay. Another tunnel collapsed just after we walked over the top."

There is no time to think of the dead—that will have to come later. When we can have a fire and remember those we will not see again. I head over to Wolf's side. "It isn't just water that's going to be a problem."

Wolf turns to face me. So does Skye and a few other of the Rogues. Glancing around, I think everyone looks stunned, exhausted and…and hurting. But we have to face the danger—Wolf and the other Rogues have taught me that.

Pushing back my shoulders, I wet my lips. "The ground shaking—it wasn't just ground shaking. I'm certain we felt the AI's first test at getting the Norm ready to leave this world."

Bird mutters something I can't quite hear and a few others sit up, but I keep my stare on Wolf. "The AI is still active and when she finishes making the Norm into her spaceship, she's going to leave nothing but destruction in her wake. We're running out of time to stop her."

# Chapter Three

Wolf wants to call a council meeting, but four of the council are missing. Crow argues we should worry more about water than anything else. I am not sure that's true—the AI wants all of us dead and this world gone. That is the big worry. But Crow is right about one thing—without water, we cannot fight the AI. Wolf agrees to a few attempts to get back into the tunnels to any who might be alive and whatever supplies we can find. But the ground shakes again, knocking me off my feet and leaving others gasping.

Where the tunnels were, the ground is a deep scar—a black gash. Throat tightening, I climb to my feet and try not to think of those buried. The tunnels no longer exist.

"That's it—we can't stay here," Wolf says. When Croc starts to protest that some can't travel, Wolf slashes a hand through the air. "We have to go. Get them ready."

We carry what few things we have and head to the ATs, but there is no good news there. Boulders have fallen, crushing all but one of the ATs—the one Skye and I took to the Empties. We can at least pull water off the crushed vehicles, but four skins and two holders are all we get. Wolf tells Croc to use the one good AT to carry those who are hurt. The rest of us walk.

Wolf leads the way to an open space where there are a few plants and only a few flat rocks. The ground dips low here—there are no tunnels, nothing but a huge, dark sky that sparkles with

19

glittering lights. We string up the covers from the ATs, using long sticks and ropes to make a cover over our small camp. I keep looking over my shoulder, waiting for a black drone to appear or for a scab to lurch up over the horizon, heading toward us from the Norm. Instead the night is oddly quiet. Only the wind whispers. No animals seem to be out tonight. With the sun down, the air cools.

Crow and Pike take the first watch. Though we haven't seen any drones or scabs, the AI could be waiting for us to be out in the open like this before attacking. Everyone seems uneasy. Wolf allows Croc to build a small fire, and I try to help Croc as much as I can with those hurt, but he sends me away to rest.

I can't sleep. Lying on the cooling sand, I keep thinking about the AI.

How long will it take her to get the Norm ready to leave? Is it ready now and are these ground shakers going to get worse? If these are tests, then when the AI pulls the Norm from this world, I fear the ground will split apart. How are we going to stop the AI? She has shut down all access, which leaves us unable to attack her. So what can we do?

I keep circling around that idea and finally give up on sleep. Standing, I brush the dust from the thin leathers I wear—just like the other Rogues—and head to where I can see Wolf's dark form silhouetted against the night sky.

Others are unable to sleep as well. I see Bird and Skye sitting close together. Bird's hair ribbon's flutter in the night breeze.

Skye rests her head in Bird's lap and speaks so softly I can only make out her high-pitched voice but not the words. She sounds sad, like maybe she is shedding tears. It's a clear night and the moon is rising in a huge disc that washes pale light over the Outside. It's almost beautiful. A night bird gives a call and small, ground animals that I hear but can't see scurry out of my path as I make my way to Wolf's side.

Wolf sits on a rock near the edge of the canvas covering, keeping watch. I sit next to him, close enough that the heat from his body warms me. Close enough to smell his scent—something musky and…nice

"Where were you today?" Wolf asks. His voice is low and deep and he sounds tired. I bite my lip and shrug. Wolf nods. "The Empties. Why do you keep going back? Not much left."

I shrug again and shift a little closer to him. The night is getting cold. "I…I don't know. Maybe…it's because I'm like the AI. It could be Bird's been right all along. Maybe it's the AI that makes me want to go there. Maybe that's how she made me."

Wolf shakes his head and glances at me. I feel his movements more than see them. "Bird's right about a lot of things, but what shapes us most are our choices. The AI doesn't make your choices, Lib. You do."

I dig the toe of my boot into the sand. "I wish I could be sure. I…Wolf, I wasn't born. I'm not even a real Glitch. I don't know what the AI imbedded into me, but—what if I do become a tool of the AI? What if I'm that and I don't even know it. It is possible

21

that the biogear was something the AI wanted me to create to make me more like—"

Wolf puts a finger over my lips. I shiver, but stop talking. He takes his finger away and he brushes a strand of my hair back over one ear and away from my face. "You think too much."

I don't know what to say to that so I remain silent. Tension seems to hang in the air between us, but it's not a bad one. Wolf reaches over and takes my hand in his. My heart jumps and thuds against my ribs. I'm surprised, but don't pull away. Despite the calluses on his fingers, his hand—big and warm—feels good.

"We need help," he says.

Frowning, I ask, "Like from the Rejects in the Norm? They got us out of the Norm last time. Do you think they can help us now? But How?"

He runs his free hand through his hair. "Look around, Lib. We've lost too many to go up against the AI again. We need to reach out to the other clans."

"Why don't you sound like that's a good thing?"

Letting go of my hand, he stands and faces me. "I'll send Crow and Bird ahead. Clans—not every Rogue clan wants to give help. Some clans…they don't share and they don't like others in their territory. But we need help."

I tilt my head to the side. I've heard mention of other clans but I never really thought I would meet any, and haven't given the other clans much thought. Bird, I know, came from the Sees Far Clan. But I've been told most of the Rogue clans aren't friendly toward Glitches. It seems some aren't even friendly to other Rogues. Will they see me as a Glitch since I was thrown out of the Norm? Like any Glitch, I can hack the Norm…or I used to be able to hack the platforms when they had power.

Standing, I put my hand on Wolf's arm. "If our choices do shape us, this sounds like a big one to make. If we're not welcome—"

"I'll make sure we are. I have favors to collect."

I pull my hand away. "This is a distraction, Wolf. Maybe it's what the AI wants—to drive us away from the Norm, keep us from going after her while she's weak. We've been hanging back, waiting for her to make the next move. But what if—"

"Lib, the Tracker Clan lost its council. We have little water, we have what food we'll be able to scavenge and we have no safety. We don't even have time to remember the dead properly. You can't ask more from the clan now. It's survival first—then we figure out what to do about the AI, if there is anything to do."

I step back. "I can't ask more? You want to talk survival, well the fight with the AI is about if we live or die. And if you want choices—running away is never a good one."

Wolf stares down at me and I stare up at him. The silence stretches between us and it is no longer warm or comfortable. Wolf's priority has always been his clan. But I thought he understood that no one is going to survive if Conie leaves this world with the Norm.

But he's still a Rogue first and last.

23

A lump tightens in my throat. I don't seem to have a choice here—except to go with the clan.

"Maybe you're the one who needs to think more." I mutter the words and turn away from him. Wolf doesn't try to stop me.

And I start to wonder if I am going to have to face the AI on my own—but how?

# Chapter Four

The night gives me too much time for thinking. Sleep seems a bad idea. I still remember the dreams I used to have after I'd been thrown out of the Norm, the ones where black tar dripped into the tunnels and flooded them, swallowing up the clan. I remember the voice calling to me, telling me I was doing a good job. And I can remember how good it felt to hear that familiar voice—the AI's voice.

Conie.

I hadn't known it was the AI. I don't know how she could do that. A connection to my memories? Or a more direct connection to me? She wanted to control me, to use me to find the Glitches and Rogues for her. She wanted them gone because they were taking resources she needed. I wonder now if she doesn't want to go without first completing that mission.

Sitting with my back to the warm rocks and my butt on cooling sand, I turn my thoughts to the conversation with Wolf. It is easier to deal with. The idea of meeting other Rogues has some merit—we could use help. But it was hard enough to convince the Tracker clan to go against the AI. And does Wolf simply want food and shelter for his clan?

I push that thought away. Wolf has fought the AI with me—he knows we must win this battle. But I can see his point. Without the tunnels, without food and water, we are at the mercy of the

Outside—and it is far too easy to die in the harsh heat and hard lands. Staring at the eastern sky, I wait for the sun to rise.

I don't want to be at odds with Wolf—I like him too much for that. And I know he has feelings for me. Those little touches he gives me, the way he presses his mouth to mine as if stealing the breath from me. That means something. But I cannot let feelings stop me from doing what I must do to defeat the AI.

In some ways, I envy Wolf. He has his clan. He knows who he is. He was born a Rogue in the Outside.

But me? Maybe I'm something like the AI inside with a shell made of flesh and blood. It would explain how the AI seems to get inside my head. It would explain the dreams and the things that I couldn't possibly know or remember.

"I feel human," I mutter. Even as I say it to myself, I can't shake the thought when it comes.

*That could just be your programming.*

Lifting a hand, I stare at my fingers, open and close them. My skin seems pale in the moonlight. The sand seems hard underneath me. Are these sensations just part of some program to observe? Am I different because I don't just act on my feelings? Because I have to think everything through?

I do not want to be the AI's ultimate weapon—but I am uncertain if there is a choice in that.

Hearing soft voices, I stare into the darkness. Slowly, I make out Bird's fluttering ribbons. The darker shadow next to her moves—it's Wolf. He puts a hand on her shoulder. My throat tightens and I turn away. They do belong together in a way I do not. With Bird, Wolf can be the kind of leader the Tracker clan wants.

Sighing, I lie down and stare up at the stars. I still won't sleep, but at least I won't have to watch Wolf and Bird.

*     *     *

The sun hasn't even warmed the sand or peaked over the mountains, and already the clan is rising, starting to deal with the day. Mostly that means scavenging some roots we can eat. Crow boils water to make a broth, and Croc is tending to those hurt.

Wolf heads to the rock where I found him sitting last night. He stands on it and raises his arms. "Make ready to travel. Bird and Pike will drive ahead to find other clans. Croc will travel with the ATs and those hurt. We'll head to the Glass Hall. It's neutral ground where we can regroup and there is water and food kept there just for such an emergency as this."

Murmurs ripple through the clan. Glancing around, I see a few nodding. Some look at the ground, mouths pulled down, as if they cannot bear to leave those we must leave buried. I also see a few nervous glances—they're worried about seeking help from other clans, too.

My stare lands on Bird. She doesn't look surprised or nervous. I wonder if she had a vision about meeting with other clans. I don't really understand Bird's visions. I tried once to follow her path, to have my own vision, but I am not really certain that I did. Now Bird stares at Wolf and nods, as if she agrees with everything he said. She wants to give up the fight with the AI—I know that suddenly and with a calm certainty. She holds influence with the clan—if she backs from the fight, I might really be on my own. Looking around, however, I see Alis and two other Glitches. Maybe I can rely on their help? Wolf jumps down from the rock, but calls out, "Take as many supplies as you can. Move fast, move light."

That's a Rogue saying.

Instantly, the clan starts to move. Everyone seems to know what to do. Several of the clan move to help Croc get those injured to the two ATs we still have. Others move away, gathering sticks that can be turned into walking staves or into weapons. I have no idea what I should do.

Heading to join Skye and Alis, I stand next to them—they don't seem to know what to do, either. Alis must still be grieving Dat, as I am. I keep glancing around, expecting to see his bright eyes and curly hair. But that will never happen again. Skye's eyebrows lift up as I come over to her side. Alis flashes me a tired smile—dark smudges shadow her eyes.

Alis leans over and asks, "This joining up with another clan—is that really going to work?"

I shrug, unsure what to answer. I don't want to admit I'm worried.

My silence seems to frustrate Alis, because she makes a low growl and demands, "Whose side are you on, Lib?"

I turn to face her. "Side? There's only the fight against the AI, Alis."

She shakes her head. Dust from the tunnel collapse clings to her hair, darkening it from red to brown. "There are always sides. And do you really think other Rogues are going to listen to you about attacking the AI?"

Her cheeks redden. She turns away and strides over to the ATs where Croc is trying to figure out how he can get them to hold everyone who is hurt. I fear we may have to leave some behind, but would Wolf even allow that?

Skye glances from Alis back to me, but she doesn't throw in her opinion. Her blue eyes linger on me for a moment and she mutters something about helping to pack what little food and water we have. She turns and walks away.

I follow after Skye, dragging my boots in the sand..

Water is passed around, but we only get two sips each. Even with that, the water will not go very far.

I hear the crunch of a heavy step and turn. Wolf heads to my side. I can see he wants to talk. Turning to Skye, I say, "I'll be right back."

Heading over to meet Wolf, I fall into step next to him.

He leads me away from the clan to the same place we sat last night. I find myself missing the stars. It's hot and the sun beats down on our heads.

Before he can say anything, I ask, "Is everyone going? All the wounded? And Alis and Skye? Will other clans accept Glitches?" I bite down on my lower lip. I shouldn't have to ask him this—I should know.

The look in his eyes seems to say the same thing. He shakes his head slowly. "No one's being left."

"Just the dead." The words come out before I can stop them.

Wolf's shoulders sag. "Yes. And remembering them must wait. But that's not what I need to ask you."

I tense. Is Wolf going to ask me to give up the fight against the AI?

Letting out a breath, Wolf puts a hand on my arm. "You're going to come with us?" Uncertainly leaks into his voice. I've never heard that tone from him. "You're not going to stay and try to fight on your own?"

He sounds worried...almost scared. "You care that much that you ask?" Offering him a small smile, I nod. "I thought about it, but this is my family. I want to stay with you."

He leans forward and presses his lips against mine. His lips are dry, but warmth dances through me. His tongue darts out to lick into my mouth. He smells of sweat and heat and dust. I can't deny how much I like that kiss.

It ends quickly, leaving me breathless. Wolf touches a fingertip to my cheek. "I don't think I could go without you."

The warmth inside me spreads up and out. "I know. But…Wolf, when we find the other clans, we have to speak of the AI. About fighting Conie. We have to."

His smile drops away. He turns and walks away. And I start to wonder if it really would be better for me to stay and fight the AI.

# Chapter Five

We start the walk before sunset, something I've never seen the clan do before. We don't have enough supplies, but there's nothing to be done about that. Bird and Pike left hours ago. Croc finally figured out how to get those who cannot walk onto the ATs—two of the clan who should probably ride gave up their seats, insisting they could walk. And they do.

Alis, Skye and I keep to the back of the group, even though I want to walk up front where Wolf leads. But I do not feel like a leader—to me it seems I keep dragging the clan into battles that we keep losing.

How long has it been since I felt invincible? Was that just the biogear that made me feel that way? Now all I can think is how foolish that was.

"What exactly is this Glass Hall?" Alis asks. She hefts the bag of food and a few pieces of gear she managed to pull out of the collapsed tunnels. I've never heard of the place, so I look to Skye.

With a shrug, Skye says, "It's underground just like the other tunnels, but from what I understand, it is an older place. Something more like the Empties."

Alis snorts. "Rogues work with dirt, rock and sand. How much better can this place really be? Is it really glass?"

Giving Alis a sideways look, Skye shakes her head. "I don't know. I've never seen it—it's a Rogue place. I'm actually surprised we're heading there with the clan."

"Wolf said no one gets left. Of course we're all going. You're part of the Tracker clan. End of story."

The sun sets, but the air is still warm. A breeze tugs at my hair, ruffling it and swirling sand. If it gets windy, we may be caught in a sand storm. I hope not.

We keep walking, moving in almost a single file as the moon rises. Rogues never complain, but I see a few struggling to keep up, wandering off the path Wolf chooses and being dragged back by others. Wolf's back becomes a dark shadow against a purple sky. I lick my lips and wish for water—or for food or to stop and sit.

This is harder than a scavenge. On a scavenge, we'd go out, we'd have ATs to ride. We might walk some, but we would rest and stop to take water or eat. I have no idea when Wolf will let us rest, so I turn my thoughts to what the other clans might be like.

The Rogues know how to survive in the Outside—they are the ones born in the Outside. Every Rogue grows up learning what plants hold water, what animals to avoid and which ones can be hunted and eaten. It takes a Glitch to hack the Norm, but while I glimpse platforms that might offer a connect, Wolf keeps us walking.

With every dragging step, I hope this Glass Hall is like the Empties. That it is above the ground and can offer us shelter and food and water. My mouth seems dry as the dirt under my feet. Even though the air cools, sweat drips down my back.

In the distance, animals howl or snarl. Alis and Skye drop back, their steps slowing and dragging more than mine. I don't let them get out of my sight, but I'm glad to be alone with the night. I like it better this way. It seems at times that I do better on my own—that I was meant to be this way. But that is also a frightening thought. What if I am singular—what if I belong nowhere other than with the AI that would rather have me dead?

Ahead of me, I spot Crow. His tall, thin frame stands out amid the other Rogues. He seems tireless, but keeps his long stride short enough that he stays with the rest of the clan.

Letting my stride lengthen, I catch up to Crow and fall in beside him. Crow glances at me, but it is too dark to see his expression. "Walking well?" he asks.

It's a Rogue phrase. The answer should be, 'well enough.' I am too tired to give even that answer. In the darkness, I can't see the scar that slashes down one side of his face. I can only see his strong nose in profile and the flash of moonlight from high cheekbones. I'm grateful for his friendship, even though something inside tells me it has shifted for him.

He nudges me with his shoulder and leans down. "You're the only company I want to keep."

Forcing a smile, I jab an elbow into his ribs and tell him, "Sometimes I feel like I don't have a lot of friends—I don't want to lose you as a friend." I glance at him to see if he understands my meaning, but I still can't gauge his reaction. Does he understand I need him as only a friend?

We walk in silence for a time, saving our breath to make it up a hillside. On the top, I ask, "Have you been to the Glass Hall?"

"Once. I was pretty small, but I remember it. There are few reasons for the clans to collect, and one of the big ones is when another clan disappears or is almost destroyed, like the See Far Clan." He falls silent for a moment, and then shakes his head. "That was a bad time."

*Bird's clan.*

Will Bird and Pike really be able to find the other clans? Will they meet with us? A twinge of sadness tightens in my chest for Bird—no wonder she is touchy about some things. No one deserves to lose their family. I ask Crow, "You remember that?"

He nods, but keeps his focus ahead of us. Going down a hillside can be more work than going up—rocks can slide from underfoot, and the clan moves carefully now. "Gatherings are a time for those who want to leave a clan to be able to shift. I wasn't born Tracker. My mother came from the Fighter Clan."

That makes sense to me—a clan would become too inbred if some shifting between clans was not allowed. But I ask Crow, "Your clan—your birth clan—it was named for your skills?"

He nods. "That and because my mother's clan didn't believe in getting along with anyone—they fight anyone, even other clans."

"What? Why?"

We move out onto level ground. Crow's stride lengthens and I have to work harder to keep up. He shifts the sack of supplies he carries on his shoulder. "Who knows? Resources, pride, fear. My mother made her choice, but I didn't have a say in it. She asked for me to be allowed to leave our clan, and then whatever clan would accept me, that's where I went."

Frowning, I stare at the ground. We skirt the edges of mountains now, keeping away from prickly bushes. "I don't understand. Why did she ask for you to leave?"

"My father was killed during a fight with another clan. It…changed my mother. She told me she didn't want me growing up fighting other Rogue clans."

"But why wouldn't you have a choice? I don't think of belonging to a clan as being a prisoner. And why didn't she come with you?"

His stare seems focused on the horizon for a long moment. At last, he glances at me, but his face is lost in shadows. His voice sounds a little tired and a little amused. "When you've been in a clan for most of your life, it's hard to leave. Traditions are part of it. Each clan is a little different, so it's difficult to adjust to something new. When you're young, change isn't so hard."

The wind picks up and slaps my face with cold air. I push back my hair and ask Crow, "Do you miss her?"

"I did. But I hardly remember her now."

Shock chills me. I was pushed from the Norm—just as Crow was pushed from his family. But now he hardly remembers them. Is this why the Tracker Clan tries to remember those who die? So they will not become hard and brutal like the Fighter Clan? And are there other clans as dangerous as that one?

36

Looking up ahead to Wolf's huge, dark shape, it seems to me the Tracker Clan is lucky to have him to lead. But what are we going into? Will the Fighter Clan come to the Glass Hall, too? From the sound of it, if they do, there won't be any fighting, but Crow makes me wonder if this other Rogue clan should even be trusted.

I'm about to ask more questions, but the wind slaps at me, stealing away my words. Sand scrapes over my skin. It is too dark to see if the bushes are bending, but I have learned to read these sights.

Sand in the air means trouble. Wolf stops, and so do the others. The wind turns wild, swirling. Looking up, I can still see the moon but the sky is turning dark.

Crow leans down and calls out, "Sandstorm!"

Wolf lifts a hand and turns to the mountains. He scrambles up the hillside and seems to disappear, but keeps yelling out to everyone, telling them to hurry. The rest of the clan follows. After glancing back to make sure Alis and Skye can see us, I follow Wolf's shouts. Wind stings my face. I have to squint and when I breathe in, I gulp down sand.

White cliffs rise up in front of me, dotted with black holes. Caves, I hope. I also hope no animals are taking shelter here.

The dust leaves me squinting. The wind pulls at my shirt and pants and seems to try to push into every part of my body. It is as if the world is turning into nothing but dust and wind. It bites at me and pulls the moisture from my eyes and mouth.

Tiny grains of sand pepper my skin, stinging like the bites of insects. If we don't get to the caves, the clan will scatter and be lost. Storms like this are more dangerous than any predatory animal or even more dangerous than the heat of the sun.

Can we get to the caves in time?

Falling to the ground to try and get below the pushing wind, I scrape my fingers on the rocks as I struggle to get to safety. I have no time to worry now for Alis and Skye—I might not make it to the caves.

I can hear Wolf yelling, using his voice to guide the clan to safety. Looking up and squinting, I can barely see his tall, dark shape through the blowing sand. The air seems to choke me. I need a coat on or a scarf over my face, but I lack those things. Every breath is a struggle and hurts my chest. I feel as if I am being buried alive now.

I want to yell to Wolf to tell him to help me—to keep shouting. I want to look back and wait for Alis and Skye. But the wind steals any words I shout and now I see nothing but dust.

The dust swirls around me. All I can do is keep clawing at rock, keep climbing. Something grabs my arm. I let it. If an animal has me, I don't care. Sand fills my mouth, leaving me coughing and choking. When I can blink and see again, I stare into a cave lit now by a torch.

Wolf holds the torch high. He lets go of my arm and turns to drag others into the cave. I stagger toward the back, counting heads. Most of the clan is either leaning against the cave walls, coughing even harder than I am, or have sat down in the dirt, shoulders slumped. They all look exhausted and dirty. Crow trudges deeper into the cave. Alis and Skye stagger out of the dark night, windblown and fall to the dirt floor. The tightness in my chest eases—we are all here. Even Croc, who helps the wounded to the back of the cave. But we seem to have lost our last two ATs.

*     *     *

Outside, the wind howls. The clan gathers at the back of the cave, which is shallow and smells of bear. Wolf's torch is growing weak, but we have no other wood. Most of the clan is already asleep. The day has been long. I sit with my arms around my knees and my back to the wall, listening to the wind. Every now and then a gust sneaks inside the cave, slapping me with sand and cold.

Skye sleeps curled up with her head pillowed on her arms. Alis sleeps sitting upright next to me. Looking at her, I can't help thinking about Dat who sometimes seemed like Alis' shadow. I know now what it must have been like for him to feel the dirt filling his lungs, to know the desperation of death coming closer. I want to remember him and mourn him, but I wonder also if he is one of the lucky ones. He will never have to face thirsty or hunger, or the AI's fury.

I am thirsty, hungry and unwilling to sleep for fear of dreams. Pushing to my feet, I see Crow's head come up. He watches me, but says nothing and doesn't beckon me over. I'm grateful. He's not the person I'm looking for right now.

I find Wolf sitting next to the fading light of the torch he holds. Dark circles bruise the skin beneath his eyes. His mouth pulls down in a slight frown, but he looks good enough to me.

He seems strong. Determined. Safe.

I put my back against the wall, slide down to sit and lean against him.

He glances over at me. "Water?"

I shake my head. I want some, but I know others will need it more. "Not now. Will the sun be up soon?"

Wolf makes a face, but says, "Soon."

He always knows these things. Shifting to move a pebble out from under my butt, I ask, "Is a meeting of the clans like a Tracker council meeting? I mean, do you all talk, or do you just have leaders talk?"

He rubs at his eyes—they must feel as gritty as mine do. "Depends on how many clans come. Bird should be able to get two clans—maybe Pike will get the others."

I consider his words and try to measure mine carefully in response. "How many clans are there?"

He shrugs. "No one counts. I know of four. There may be more. Some clans never come out to meet anyone, but you can see traces of them—tracks from scavenges or bones from hunts."

I wait for one breath, and then blurt out the question I've been wanting to ask, "What about speaking to the other clans about the AI?"

Wolf holds very still. His dark eyes lock onto mine. My chest seems frozen. I lick my lips. I hope he is not angry, but I have to know if Wolf is giving up the fight against the AI.

His frown deepens, and finally he says, "What do you want to tell them? How we were beat? How we had to run?"

I stiffen and stand up. "We got into the Norm. We...Raj's program might have damaged the AI. We haven't seen the Norm active. We have to tell them the truth."

He comes to his feet in a slow face move and blocks me from moving away. "And once you tell the clans this, then what? You want to ask for their help? For them to fight and die?"

Face burning, I face him. "Why not? Better to die fighting—isn't that the Rogue way?"

He winces like I've struck him. "Even better to live. Lib, I won't lead Rogues to certain death. You have a plan, let me know. Then we can talk to the clans."

"In other words, figure out a way to fight first. What if the best plan is to get all the clans to join against the AI? But that's not something you want to ask them to do, is it? Why not? Are you afraid the Fighter Clan will take the lead? That the Tracker Clan might have to work with an enemy clan?"

He reaches for my hand, but I jerk back. He makes a frustrated sound in his throat. "Why are you being so difficult?"

I stare at him. Part of me wants desperately to give in to him—to just let someone else take over this fight. But, somehow, I am a creation of the AI. Whether birthed in a womb or in some test tube, I know in my heart that I am whatever she made me to be. And Conie said I am the salvation of humanity. There is no escaping that. I can never give up this fight.

Letting out a sigh, I shake my head. "I don't want to argue anymore. But I am not giving up on this."

"Even if this battle may take all of the clans, and it may cost all our lives?"

All I can do is nod, for somehow we must stop the AI—and we have to save those in the Norm from Conie.

# Chapter Six

The next morning, sand fills half the entrance to the cave. We have to climb out over the dust and into the harsh light. We have time to drink a few sips of water and eat some of the dried meat. We need more supplies. The sky is a pale blue and in the distance I can see the curving edge of the Norm—we are walking around it, I realize. We once tried to find the far side of the Norm, but it is too vast for that. But now I can see a new part of it—the metal shines in the light, almost blinding.

We start out before it is too hot, coming down from the cliff and walking with the Norm to one side and the cliffs to the other.

At the hottest part of the day, Wolf calls a halt, and we find a little shelter under the cliff overhangs. As everyone settles into whatever shade they can find, Wolf jogs over to me. I glance up, a little surprised he is coming over to me.

He stops in front of me and asks, "Think you can find a platform?"

"A working one?" I ask. I shrug. "Maybe."

He nods. "Take Skye. I'm taking Crow and Mouse to see if we can find any plants with water in them. Maybe dig up some roots."

I nod. The plants with water—the cactus—seem to be harder and harder to find. But a lot of the scrub plants have soft, tasty roots. I glance at Crow, who stands behind Wolf, frowning and rubbing at the scar on his face. He shakes his head as if he thinks the idea of trying to scavenge any food is useless.

Turning back to Wolf, I push my shoulders back. "We'll try." I wish I had more than Skye going with me, but when I glance at Alis, she sits with her shoulders slumped and her pale skin turning pink. She doesn't look as if she'll be of much use. I nod and tell Wolf, "We'll follow after you when we get the supplies."

*If we can scavenge anything from the nearest platform.*

Wolf drags a hand through his dark hair. "The clan can't stay here long. Only until the sun starts to go down."

I nod. "I know."

His mouth pulls down. "Be careful." He puts a hand on my shoulder. Warmth spreads through my body. I put my hand over his, and then turn and head out to find Skye.

But I am not certain we'll be able to scavenge anything from the Norm—the AI has it locked up tight.

\*     \*     \*

It seems to take forever to find a platform, but Skye spots one at last, and points to the sunlight glittering off the railing and metal panels. Even if this goes as smoothly as I hope, we won't be able to carry much with us. But some water is better than none.

Skye perks up as we head to the platform, but we're both keeping an eye on the sky, looking for drones or scabs. Nothing shows up.

The platform looks like an old one. One pillar is half rusted and hanging down. The roof sags. The floor looks clogged by sand and faded from the sun. I step up to the railing—that seems intact. Skye puts a hand on my arm. "Are you sure you want to try a hack?"

I shake my head. "We need water. And…well, this is not the first time the two of us have worked together. What is the problem? Do you think something will go wrong?"

Skye drops her hand and rubs the back of her neck. "First the AI seems like it's dead, then it shakes the earth—that was the AI, wasn't it? So… how safe is it to go poking around inside the AI with a connect?"

With a shrug, I wave at the railing that will let me connect. "When has this ever been safe?"

Skye lets out a long breath. She wets her lips—she is as thirsty as I am, but I also share her worries. She pulls a face and says, "I…we've made the AI into an enemy. This is a lot more dangerous than it used to be."

I glance at the railing. Will the AI know I've connected? Or did Raj's code damage Conie's core? I realize my palms are sweating, but I also really want a peek inside—if I can get one. "I'm not stupid enough to think that I can sneak by the AI without any sort of detection. She's always watching—but we might not even be able to make a connect."

Skye backs up a step. "I almost wish that's true. Make it quick."

She turns and walks away. For a moment, I can only stare at her back and her long hair, being pulled by the wind. Something has changed inside her. She no longer even wants to try a connect—she seems to freeze up over the idea. We've saved each other's lives, but we've also grown apart and I don't know why.

Taking a breath, my feet planted wide on the platform, I put my palm against the railing. For a moment, nothing happens. The metal is warm—and nothing sparks. I should feel a prick against my palm. I close my eyes—and open them only to find myself still standing on the platform.

I hate this.

And I decide I am done playing by the AI's rules. I am going to force a connect.

I yank the railing out, exposing bare wiring. Light flashes along one wire. I grab it.

Closing my eyes, I will myself into the system—I have no biogear, but I am certain now I don't need it. My biogear exists inside me. For a moment, I only feel sweat sticking my shirt to my back. I hear only the wind singing through the metal of the platform. I let that fade, and focus not on my hand, but on the thin thread deep inside me—the one that tugs me into dreams.

My heartbeats slows. My breathing seems to stop. The wire in my hand warms.

I open my eyes.

I stand in a world of cool blue, endless walls. Familiar lines of filing cabinets to my left and right go on endlessly in front of me.

And behind me. I wait, my breath tight in my chest, or that is how it feels even in this artificial world. Will Conie send scabs after me—or sentinels who act as virtual guards.

The room seems paler than usual—and I hear no sounds.

I summon a screen, will it to exist and begin my search.

*Water.*

Code dances over the screen, lines of information that is somehow something I understand. The information temps as it always does—I always want to know more. But I must focus. The clan needs water and we need it in containers Skye and I can carry.

The hairs on the back of my neck prickle. This is taking too long. And then an image jumps out of the code and I stop the search.

*Raj.*

Trembling, I don't know if I want to know more, but I cannot resist. I have to know.

I expand the image and see Raj's face. He looks tired, his dark skin an odd gray and his dark, curly hair seems shorter than it used to be.

He stares at me, and his voice echoes in my head. *If you've found this, then I'm dead. Or worse. I know that's hard on you, Lib, but you're going to have to let it go. There are other things at stake. You know what's most important.*

My throat tightens and my heart thuds in my chest with dull, heavy beats. I want to call out to him, but I know I can't. This is just some of Raj's hidden code. A message he left just in case I came back for him.

*This isn't your fault, whatever's happened to me. I made my own choices. I don't regret them. What you need to know is that the AI is going to launch the Norm soon. Testing has started and things are going to get bad. You have to stop it, Lib. You're the only one who can.*

Raj's message ends. The screen goes back to lines and lines of code scrolling past. I clench a fist. I want to go after him—I want to find him and get him out of here. But Raj is right—it is too late.

Raj can't come back. If he is not dead, he is part of the system. Conie has integrated him.

Reminding myself that I have a job to do, I resume the search for water. I find access, and revise the code. We have no containers, so I need the water to be pulled from the Norm and delivered to the platform. That's more risky than anything else. Once I'm done, I shut down the screen and step back.

With a blink, I'm back in the Outside, my palm tingling. The wire is cold now and dead. I'm left wondering how I forced this connect. I open and close my hand. I have more power than I know, and it almost frightens me. But, to defeat the AI—to really beat Conie—I may have to access the parts of me that she wanted to hide from me.

Glancing over, I see Skye watching with huge, blue eyes. She hugs herself and stays away from me. "You were in there a long time—that wasn't quick."

I wince. "It is what it is."

Skye drops her arms to her sides. "Any longer and I was going to have to get in there to get you out." She sounds angry—and worried.

And I suddenly know Skye wouldn't have been able to make the connect. Not here and not now. I glance at my hand again. I forced this connect—it wasn't a normal one. I shouldn't have been able to hack a connect with just one wire.

Glancing at Skye, I tell her. "Water's coming."

Skye frowns. "Coming from where?"

I step out of the creaking platform. It feels as if it's ready to fall apart. The sun is hot after the cool blue of the artificial world. I keep my head down to avoid the glare. And I listen.

"It's quiet." I whisper the words.

Skye starts to nod, but stops and lifts her head. She turns and her face pales.

"Drone," I tell her quietly. "It's bringing the water. Stay low and stay next to the platform. Don't think. Don't move. Don't breathe."

Skye glances at me. She doesn't move, so I grab her hand and drag her against one of the platform pillars and push her against it. I stand next to the pillar opposite her. If she moves, she's dead.

The drones move in fast, going from a black dot in the sky to a humming black orb.

I hold my breath and try to lock stares with Skye, but she is staring at the ground.

*Don't move. Don't move.*

Willing Skye to stay where she is, I hold myself still and send images out of the platform empty and dusty.

The drone stops over the platform. It sinks down and rotates seeming as if to face me.

*Nothing here. Empty platform.*

I keep sending the images, pushing them out as I pushed out the connect. If Conie can invade my dreams, I should be able to use that thread to push back—to send images.

Something slides open on the drone's black sphere and it extends one thin arm.

*Water. Leave water. Prime command.*

The drone reaches inside its sphere and pulls out one container and then another and then another and then a fourth. It settles them on the sand. Skye shifts a tiny bit. The drone whirls, a red light blinking on.

*Shadow—play of light. Return. Now!*

I slam out the last order, staring at the drone, willing myself into its circuits and code. For a second, the world becomes virtual—I see pale blue and connections and orders flowing past in bursts of light. For a moment, it seems as if I will be sucked into this world—I can get lost here in information. And I want that—I want to know more.

A crash and the spit of dying circuits pulls me from that other place. Blinking, letting out the breath I'd been holding, I see Skye standing over the drone. It's glowing red eye fades to black. Skye holds one of the platform poles in her hand. Behind her, the platform creaks and falls into the sand. The drone's eye starts to glow again and Skye slams the metal pole down on it, battering it to pieces.

When she's done, I walk over and kick at the gear. "It was going to leave."

Skye drops the piece of metal. "How do you know?"

I shake my head. How do I tell her that for an instant, I was the drone? I was inside it. I was connected without even touching it.

I shiver.

The done is dead. I wave at Skye to grab two of the containers. When I lift the other two, my arms protest. They're heavy. But I don't want to give up a drop.

I also don't want to think about the things I have learned about myself today. But I will have to face them soon enough—and I will have to learn how to focus these new skills. If I can.

# Chapter Seven

We struggle, but get the water back to the clan. The containers leave my hands sore and my shoulders aching. But everyone is happy to see us. Wolf and the others also scavenged two huge lizards, three snakes and a rabbit as well as roots. We eat that night—not enough to fill my stomach, but some. I watch the sky, but no more drones come out.

But I still keep watch.

The next morning Skye seems distant and unhappy so I sit next to her and ask, "What's wrong?"

She lifts one shoulder and seems reluctant to answer, but eventually admits, "I'm not sure I want to meet the other Rogues."

I open my mouth to reassure her, but nothing comes out. I thought she was still thinking of the connect. Instead, she looks to the future, and I have no idea what to say. We don't have long to eat—and there is not much to fill us, so we start to walk again.

In the distance, I notice familiar shapes jutting up into the sky like dark spires warning of past destruction. But the Empties I know lie in another direction. Catching up to Crow, I ask, "What is that?"

He glances at me. "You thought there was only one set of Empties? There are lots of them scattered around. I hear the Empties once covered most of the land."

My jaw slackens. "Lots of Empties," I mutter. Have I been looking in the wrong set of Empties all this time for my answers?

"These…the ones with the Glass Hall, they're like neutral territory for clans." He chooses his words like he tastes them first to see if they feel right. "There used to be a lot more clans, and more clan wars. Got bad enough, fighting over what we could get from the Empties, that something had to give."

"If the clans all want what they can get from the Empties, why meet there?"

He grins, and the scar on the side of his face seems to twist his mouth on one side. "Might as well meet at one of the places where every Rogue came from."

I think about all the times I've traveled to the Empties—or to the Empties nearest the Tracker Clan. I've been searching for answers, but what if my answers are in the Glass Hall?

Suddenly, I'm eager to get to this place.

*     *     *

It seems the Empties are all alike.

Paths of hard blackness dusted by the wind cut between towering buildings of twisted metal. But I see why they call this place the Glass Hall. Everything seems to be made of glass. Dusty as it is, the glass still reflects back our images. The Rogues look like scavengers—skin clothing hangs ragged from their arms and legs. Dusty boots held together with plant twine cover their

53

feet. Everyone's hair is windblown and tangled. I stare at myself—how very long ago it was that I had on a smooth tunic from the Norm and was clean and pale?

All of it this is familiar to me, but these Empties are also different.

Metal still clings to spots, rusting and forgotten. Things that look like huge ATs sit here. The Empties of the Glass Hall have not been scavenged by the clans into complete emptiness.

We move slowly—we can only go as fast as our injured can move. Croc and Wolf help those who limp along. A few stare up at the towers around us as if they have never seen this place—and maybe they haven't.

It seems to me that I see wonder and a touch of fear in almost everyone's face—except for Wolf. He walks with his eyes straight ahead and his back stiff, as if he does not trust this place. I find it fascinating.

There is little sound—just the crunch of our boots on the sand and the debris. I search for drones or scabs, but it seems the AI has no use for any of the Empties.

We walk deeper into the Empties, and I begin to see differences. The Empties of the Glass Hall have no trees or plants. And it seems as we move deeper, there is more destruction. Instead of standing buildings, they seem to have fallen to their sides or to have become nothing but bare, twisted metal. I wonder if Dr. Constance Sig ever visited here. I can almost imagine her standing nearby, watching as we pass.

Of course, she can't be. Dr. Sig has been dead a long time.

Wolf leads the way to a place where the ground slopes down and to a place where a rusted square of metal leads into the side of what looks like a square, gray mountain.

He motions for the clan to stop, and he steps forward and shouts, "We come to meet. To speak of our survival. The Tracker Clan comes to meet."

I glance around. Who is he talking to?

The rusted metal opens—it is a door. I cannot see inside, it is too black, and no one comes out.

Wolf glances back at the clan and then gestures to the half-open door. "I'm going in to find Bird and Pike. After I come back, we'll go in together as a clan." His eyes flicker to me. He turns and then he's gone inside. The metal clangs shut.

I glance around. At least I'm with the rest of the clan. Skye winds her hair around one finger. Alis is staring at the door and frowning, and so is Crow. It seems everyone is nervous—except for Croc, who is too busy making those who are hurt comfortable to notice. I go to help him give water to those who are not doing so well. I fear we may lose a few more before long due to their injuries.

I also keep glancing at that metal door. Why isn't this Glass Hall made of glass? I find myself not wanting to go inside there—I keep thinking of the earth shaking and how it might do that again, and I do not want to be around ground that could fall on me then.

At last the metal creeks open again and Wolf walks out with Bird and Pike beside him. Those who sat down stand, and Croc and others start to ready to go inside. My heart is beating too fast. I glance at Wolf.

He comes to me and says, "Walk with me."

I frown, but nod. The clan starts to file into the doorway, into the blackness. Glancing back, I wish we were going into a glass hall instead of under the ground again. My stomach drops and I fidget with the strap to the pouch that is slung over my shoulder.

Wolf does not say anything, just watches the others as they head through the door. Crow hesitates and glances at me, his eyebrows raised. I offer him a smile and a nod to encourage him to go on through with the others. Reluctantly, he does so.

Voice low, Wolf tells me, "Bird says tensions are high. It's not just a couple of clans, all the other clans are here—all six. And four of them have lost their tunnels like we did."

I frown. "The AI—the earth shaking."

Wolf lifts a hand. "We can't know for sure. Until more is known, remain silent."

He heads inside. I realize I've clenched my jaw and I have to relax it. But I keep my lips pressed tight. Silent? How can I stay silent when everyone needs to be warned that the AI is planning to end this world?

# Chapter Eight

Stepping into the darkness is worse than a connect. For a moment, there is no light and I stumble forward, almost running into a wall. I turn a corner and then another one. And then light begins to glow.

I follow the others. We climb down a stair and then another one and then another, and then I understand why this is called the Glass Hall.

The room is massive. It's more than five times as large as the main room was in the old tunnels. The floor is a pale gray and the walls are colorless and clear. The walls are glass. In fact, everywhere there seems to be glass. Even high above, I look up and see glass that lets in light. I touch one wall and find it oddly warm and soft. I can press my hand into it and it bends but then springs back.

Looking around, some of the walls turn to a pale gray and enclose smaller rooms. It seems the glass can change to have color. It is almost like a living thing.

I also notice railings, just like those found on platforms for connects. Was this place once connected to the AI—a place where hacks were possible? Frowning, I hope not. Access to the AI also means the AI can access this place.

I reach for the railing closest to me, to touch it and see if it feels live, but Wolf calls out, "Lib."

I jerk my hand back, feeling like I've been caught doing something bad. But I'm not. I just want to make sure everyone's safe. But I wonder how this place is linked to the AI—and maybe to Dr. Sig?

Hurrying, I catch up to Wolf and fall into step just behind him. The rest of the Tracker Clam spreads out into the main room. As they do, I notice we are not the only clan here.

Four distinct groups of Rogues sprawl around the main room. Some groups seem larger—others are only about six or seven people. The different clans stand out due not so much to their faces, but what they wear.

One clan has feathers hanging from their shirts and long hair. Another has painted their skin red with what looks like clay or mud and seems to have shaved their heads, and I wonder if this is the Fighter Clan. Another group wears skins that have somehow been tanned as white as the walls in this room. The fourth wears clothes that look to be made of snake and lizard skins, for their shirts and pants rustle slightly.

*Only four?*

Are these all who would come, or are these the only clans left, along with the Tracker Clan?

As I glance at the different clan members, I notice they have a few things in common—dark skin and hard muscles. Several glance at Wolf—he seems even larger in this room—but more of them stare at me.

My face warms. I don't like all these strangers watching me. I stand next to Wolf, but he nods over to where Alis and Skye sit at the back where the Tracker Clan is settling. I know he wants me to join them.

Skye shifts from side to side, seeming uncomfortable. Alis sits with her arms crossed and something that looks like fear in her eyes.

Wolf reaches out and gives my hand a squeeze. I give him a nod and head over to sit next to Alis—Wolf must not want her causing trouble.

Wolf turns so he faces the other four clans. In front of each group, one person stands—the clan leader, I assume. One of them is a tall woman with skin painted red and hair that is little more than stubble across her skull. Her eyes seem a startling green with flashes of gold. The other three men cross their arms and glance around, almost as if daring anyone to challenge them, but I don't know why they'd think someone would.

Wolf lifts a hand and his deep voice echoes from the hard walls. "Tracker Clan lost our home and far too many of our clan, but not to drones or scabs. Not to other clans." Wolf's gaze darts to the clan with painted red skin and shorn hair. Wolf's stare doesn't linger long, but it leaves me certain that is the Fighter Clan. Wolf drops his hand to his side. "We lost everything to a shaking of the very earth."

The leader of the feather-covered clan gives a rude snort. He looks only a little older than Wolf, but he is shorter and his skin looks made almost of leather. "What concern is this to other clans? The world shakes sometimes. We all know this."

Wolf stiffens. "And is the Tracker Clan the only clan to feel the earth shake? Have you not felt it, too?"

The woman who seems to be leader of the Fighter Clan frowns and shrugs her shoulders. "What if we have, Wolf of the Tracker Clan?"

"The shaking was *not* natural. It was an attack that threatens all Rogues."

For a moment, several of the leaders speak all at once, and then other clan members start to talk. The leader of the Fighter Clan barks out a laugh.

At that, Wolf holds up a hand and slowly others stop talking. Wolf drops his hand again. "Red Kite of the Fighter Clan, you have something to say?"

When she speaks, she sounds impatient and irritable. "The Fighter Clan is not under attack—no one dares come into our territory."

Wolf's eyes flash, but he only shakes his head. "Our true enemy is the AI. And the AI dares to go where it pleases."

Red Kite's eyes narrow. Her hand drops to a knife hilt on her belt and she looks ready to snarl something at Wolf. Before she can, the leader of the clan wearing snake skins asks, "What does the AI have to do with shaking ground?"

Wolf glances at the man. "That is a good question, Mountain of the Walking Tall Clan. The Tracker Clan knows this for we have been inside the Norm." A few gasps and mutters travel around the room. Wolf ignores them. "The AI is changing the Norm and making it into a giant ship to leave this world—and destroy this world before it goes."

There's a long, strained silence, and then Red Kite barks out a laugh. More nervous laughter comes from her clan. Fists clenched, I want to get up and yell at them that they're being stupid. But they aren't the only ones. The other clans aren't laughing outright, but some in the Walking Tall clan hide smiles behind their hands. Others just shake their heads with what looks to be disbelief.

Dread knots my stomach—if the other clans doubt us, they won't help. How can we bring down the AI without their aid?

Wolf crosses his arms and his booming voices silences everyone. "Do you think Wolf of the Tracker Clan is a fool or stupid?"

The man wearing feathers on his skins lifts a hand. "Faun of the Sing-Song Clan would hear what else Wolf of the Tracker Clan has to say. Please, go on."

Mountain of the Walking Tall clan folds his arms across his chest. "Wolf sounds ridiculous. This is a story to tell the young at night."

The man wearing snake skin now lifts a hand. "Iguana of the Hills Clan would also hear what Wolf of the Tracker Clan has to say. We should at least honor him and hear him right."

I glance around—it seems Iguana of the Hills Clan, the clan in snake skins, and Faun of the Sing-Song Clan, those who wear feathers, would hear Wolf's words. But it is Red Kite of the Fighter Clan and Mountain of the Walking Tall Clan are still shaking their heads.

Iguana, who is perhaps the oldest man here, lets out a sigh, but gestures for Wolf to continue.

Wolf lifts his voice again. "Do you see the Barrow Clan here? The Fire Starter Clan? The Trade Clan? Where are they? We all know their tunnels were the deepest of all. We all know the AI has no love for Rogues."

Red Kite slashes a hand in the air in front of her. "But why would the AI wish to destroy this earth? Why not just go and leave us behind?"

I've had enough. These people must either see the truth—or they will never help us. I stand and call out into the silence, "The AI is made of alien technology, fused within it. This has left it believing aliens will return and that when they do there must be no sign of life, otherwise humanity will be in danger of being hunted down by those aliens." Wolf stiffens. Everyone seems to turn to stare at me. I stare back at them. "If you want to live, you're going to have to help us stop the AI. And I can tell you now—ground shaking is just the first part of this. The AI has the power within the Norm to split this world as if it is a ripe fruit."

Red Kite's hand drops to her knife hilt again. Mountain and Iguana stare at me. But Eagle lifts his voice and asks, "How can you know this? How can you have been in the Norm? No Rogue has ever been in there."

Pushing my shoulders back, I tell him, "Several Rogues have been in the Norm. We've met with the Rejects inside. We've seen the Techs—and I once was both a Tech and a Glitch. But now I'm Lib of the Tracker Clan and I tell you Wolf speaks the truth."

The entire room seems to erupt into noise and Rogues jumping to their feet and shouting.

# Chapter Nine

I want to clap my hands over my ears. Voices rise in anger and fear and a few of them are just shouting for everyone to sit down and be quiet. But no one is doing that. My own anger is still blazing inside me. I'm not sure any of these Rogues deserve to be saved. I sway against the noise and emotions filling the room, not really sure what to do now.

*At least they all know.*

I feel a tugging on my hand. Glancing down, I see Skye pulling on my fingers. She's still seated. She doesn't say anything—it's not like she could be heard over the crowd anyway—but she pulls on my hand as if she wants me to sit down again and stop talking.

*Too late for that.*

Mountain is shouting and pointing an accusatory finger at Wolf as if this is somehow his fault. Iguana throws up his hands and turns his back on the others, but his clan—a small one—now stands and stares around them, looking braced for a fight.

Most of the Tracker Clan is standing as well. They're shouting and waving their arms—but not against me. I can hear Crow loudly telling everyone else they're idiots if they don't believe me and Wolf. Croc is also on his feet, and so are a few of our injured. They're defending Wolf—and me.

Wolf is still on his feet, his hands up, and telling others to calm. I don't think anyone is listening to him. Not even his own clan.

Alis, like Skye, has remained seated and silent. When I glance at her, I can see she's scared. Her eyes are wide and she keeps twisting the ends of her red hair.

One shout from Red Kite can be heard over all the other noise. "I'm supposed to take the word of some half-human…thing? A Tech…a Glitch?"

*Half-human.*

The words hit like a hard punch. I stand and turn until I can see Red Kite clearly. She jabs her bare knife blade at me. "How can you know so much? What are you?"

Slowly, the room goes silent. Heads turn toward me, but I keep staring at Red Kite—at those glittering green eyes and the clay flaking from her face and the way her body quivers but her knife hand holds steady. They must be waiting for my response, but I find I have nothing to say.

I don't know what I am—not really.

The weight of my past—so much of it buried, just as the Tracker Clan tunnels were—sits on my chest like a huge slab of rock, until I struggle to breathe.

Wolf opens his mouth. Maybe he'll defend me—or maybe he'll just try to smooth things over. I don't stay to find out—I don't want to know the answer. Turning, I force myself to walk and keep walking, half blind to where I'm going.

65

Wolf said my choices define me—well, I'm making a choice now. A choice to leave this place if I can.

*     *     *

It doesn't take long for me to lose my way. Every room and hallway is either clear glass or white glass. It takes me time to slow my steps and stop walking blindly, turning down hallways just to turn down them. I stop and glance around. Why is this place so empty? So...sterile? This isn't like any other place I've known—except it is. If the walls were blue, not white, this would be like the AI's artificial world.

I start to walk again, but steps echo behind me, so I stop and turn. Alis and Skye turn the corner and stop. Alis crosses her arms. Red washes over her face. Skye shifts from one foot to the other. I motion at them to come with me. "Let's go look around while it's quiet."

Skye and Alis share a look, but head over to follow me.

We pick our way down empty corridors, peaking into rooms that hold nothing. Every now and then we find a railing, but I shy away from touching them. I just want to walk and keep walking. I'm tired of the Rogues and their arguments.

"They're a bunch of—" Alis begins, but before she can say something that is inevitably ugly and derogatory, Skye interrupts.

"They're just scared. It's hard when you're dealing with something unfamiliar."

66

I smile at her, at her calmness and her tolerance soothes.

"How much harder is it going to be when the AI leaves and wrecks this world?" Alis counters.

Skye runs her hand along one of the railings. She glances at her fingers. "Why isn't it dusty in here?"

I lift a shoulder. "Does that matter?"

Alis snorts. "Of course it doesn't. That mess we just left didn't matter, either. Talk about a waste of time."

Skye rolls her eyes. "It's odd. And odd things should be looked at. And...and doesn't this place look like inside a connect?"

With a nod, I lay my hand against the glass wall, spreading out my fingers over the cool surface. The glass reflects me—brown hair, a wide mouth, smooth skin, long, lean limbs and wide eyes. I stare at myself and then let my stare lose focus.

This does feel like inside a connect—but inside a connect, I would just imagine things to call up data. Can I do that here? When my image becomes fuzzy, a small, square image forms. I stare at it, willing it to become clear, but it seems the power is weak in this system. The image fades slightly—but if this really is like inside a connect...

Excited now, I take a deep breath and ask for a map...and the path to Dr. Sig. I choose her because I don't know who else to reference—she must have been here at some time, right? Slowly, a path forms, lighting up under my touch. Jerking my hand away,

I glance over at Alis and Skye. They're still arguing about why it's not dusty and have walked ahead of me.

I glance back at the glass and then decide to try the path just shown to me—why not, after all. I have nothing to lose. Calling to Alis and Skye, I lead them deeper into the maze of glass corridors. It is almost familiar to me—like a connect, but also like a memory. We reach a corridor that is blocked by glass.

"We should go." Alis starts to turn around, but Skye says, "I'm not sure I want to go back." She sounds unhappy. I glance at them and then take a step closer to the glass wall in front of us, I concentrate on the map shown to me. I touch the glass wall. It slides open, revealing a room. I step inside.

This room, unlike others, has a few chairs made of metal—and more glass walls. There are no tables, no gear I can see, but there's something familiar about all of this. Reaching out, I touch the nearest wall. The room brightens so the walls glow brighter. The light lets us see to find our way. On one wall, something like a screen appears.

"We're in her lab," I murmur. I don't know if that really is true, but it feels right. I must know this place because of memories that I carry from Dr. Sig—memories the AI gave me. Did she know she had done that? Was it a mistake—or something the AI could not prevent? Conie tried to hide them from me, but being here is stirring a connection to Dr. Sig that is stronger than I ever knew.

Skye comes up to stand next to me and stares at the blank screen on the glass wall. "What is this place?"

"A lab—I think. Like the Gear Room we used to have in the tunnels."

Alis walks over to the screen on the wall and touches it. She jerks her hand away. "It feels warm. Like there's power here."

Cold washes over me. Power? Why? What was this place? Why is it hidden under Empties? Did Dr. Sig hide it for a reason? Maybe to keep it hidden from the AI?

Taking a deep breath, I glance around the room. Can I access information here as I would in a connect?

I hesitate, and then reach for the screen. It is warm, but when I ask it to call up information, the screen remains stubbornly blank. Mouth pressed tight, I push my hand against the warming glass and demand access.

Bits of data start to flow, glittering lines of code that fade again.

Skye's voice sounds soft as she breaths out one word. "Wow."

"This is…more than odd," Alis says. "We should leave."

"How can you say that?" Skye says and I hear that mix of longing and anxiety in her voice. She still misses the Norm—she still wants to find a way to go back where it would be safe. She knows this place matters, too, but I think she knows more on an instinctive level.

Frowning, I focus on the screen. The screen remains dark with only blips of light, but data starts to slip into my head.

Memories flicker—only they aren't really mine, and yet they are. Random scenes that flash past almost too quickly. I grab at one.

For a flash, I see Dr. Sig reflected in the glass. She smiles at a tall man who stands next to her, his arms around the waist. I blink and the image vanishes.

Was that my family? My mother and father?

I don't know, but I do know one thing—this is Dr. Constance Sig's lab. Or it was. This is a connection to her that is separate from the AI and that might mean it has information vital to defeating the AI.

A shiver races down my spine. Pulling my hand from the warm glass, I look around the room. "Dr. Sig was here, in this room, working on technology to create the AI. But she wasn't just creating something new—she was adapting alien gear that crashed here on Earth."

Alis hugs herself. "How can you be so sure of that?"

"You did a connect?" Skye asks.

I glance from Alis to Skye—they're both looking worried. "When I was in the Norm, the AI showed me…or maybe I just was able to get glimpses…of how it was created. Dr. Sig somehow blended part of her consciousness into a machine that became the AI. It calls itself Conie—like it really is Constance Sig. But it's alien at its core. It doesn't really understand humanity, but it thinks it can protect humans without really knowing what it is protecting."

Alis glances around and hunches her shoulders. "I'm not sure I want to be here anymore."

I shake my head. "No…it's safe. This may look like a connect, but that's because the AI is using this structure for its artificial world. But this place is real. And it seems to be shielded, or at least offline from the AI's network. I'm not getting a true connect. In fact, I'm having trouble pulling up data at all. The systems are either not working right or running out of power, or maybe both."

Skye frowns. "If you're having trouble with a hack here, how do you know all this?"

I ignore her question and stare at the walls. "There must be more—and a way to access the data that could still be here."

Walking, I trail a hand over the walls, searching for other activation points. The glass goes from feeling cool to warm, and more screens appear inside the walls. I place my hand flat on one, but it remains blank. Disappointment curls inside me. The need to know is stronger than almost anything else.

I slide a hand over another screen. This one feels slightly curved. Power seems to flicker within, as if it's been so long since anyone has activated it that it is having trouble waking up, but this one seems to be in better working condition than any others. If I could just reach into it—push into a connect the way I was able to connect to a drone with just thoughts.

Closing my eyes, I push into the wiring, letting go of myself and reaching into the circuits. They are old—and mostly made of light. Bright orbs slip past me, streaking past. The power is weak—fading. It's geothermal and the vents have been cooling for so long that the system has been shutting down anything deemed unnecessary. So much has been lost—forgotten. But there is storage. Backup.

*Connection: secure.*

The backup isn't blue like the AI's construct. This connect is mostly blacks and dark hues, like the sky just after sunset. Emptiness stretches out in every direction. The back of my neck prickles, and I realize the backup holds some of the alien code—that's what I'm seeing.

The realization scares me—and it is exhilarating. How long has it been since anyone has seen this? I tread carefully, trying to unravel the dark code that speeds past me. It is almost as if the alien code has taken over all the systems—or if it is caught here in endless loops. I see the same code over and over. How is it that I was reaching for the backups and hacked this instead? Is it because the alien code needs so very little power to function?

I start to follow the lines of code, drawn by the dark, sinuous movements. It's seductive—so compact. I can sense the power within it. No wonder Dr. Sig wanted to use this. It's...elegant. New lines of code weave and form and I reach out to just touch...

"Lib?" Alis reaches out and grabs my arm. Startled, eyes flying open, I stare at her. I'd almost forgotten that she and Skye are with me.

"What?" I blurt out the word, angry for the interruption. I curl my fingers tight. Maybe Alis was smart to interrupt. I might be trying to touch things better left alone for now. But I have to know if this alien code could help us defeat the AI.

Alis and Skye share a look as if they're more than worried about me. Skye shrugs as if whatever Alis wants is nothing she is going to decide. Alis faces me and says, "We should head back or we're going to miss any kind of meal or water."

She's right. And I can always come back here. Alis turns and walks out. Skye follows, glancing back at me as if to make sure I am coming. I give one last look at the walls. The screens slowly fade away until the walls just look like glass again. Next time I'll come back on my own.

We have a little trouble finding our way back—the map is still in my head, but I am too distracted to think about it.

Back in the main room, the clans are still in their own groups, but the arguments have died down. No one looks all that happy, but no one is shouting.

Alis and Skye head straight to the area staked out by the Tracker Clan. I can smell the smoke of a fire and that seems out of place here. My stomach grumbles from the lack of food and the smell of meat roasting, but I linger in the glass hallway for a moment longer. I almost want to turn back and head to the room right now. However, maybe the screens aren't working for me because I am the one who needs rest and food.

With a heavy sigh, I head over to join the Tracker Clan. But all I can think about is the connect I had in Dr. Sig's lab.

*       *       *

After we eat, a few from the clans mingle. All except the Fighter Clan, which seems to keep to itself.

But Red Kite leaves her clan and strides across the room. Her stare locks onto me, her eyes narrow slightly, but then she grins. What does that means? Is this a challenge?

I hope not. I can fight—Wolf taught me—but I'm not sure I'd ever win against someone who has trained her entire life for combat.

Wolf is talking with other clan leaders still. I don't know what he's saying, but judging by their hard faces it isn't anything they want to hear.

I clean the little food I've been given—we still have to share what little we have—and a shadow falls across me. I glance up and see Bird standing over me.

She sits next to me and waves toward Wolf. "He's arguing that they should let you speak and tell your full story. But Red Kite won't listen to anyone now and keeps telling everyone there is no need to hold council."

I push out a breath. Wolf's fighting for me sends warm flutters through my chest, but I'm not sure he can win this fight. So why bother?

I glance at Bird. "What if I really can't be trusted and I don't even know it?"

Bird rolls her eyes. "You gave up the biogear. That counts for something." She stands and puts one hand on her hip. She's so small, yet filled with so much fire. "Your whole story can be told. All you have to do is challenge the leaders for the right. But you'd better do it before Red Kite convinces the other clan leaders that you're dangerous." I glance up at Bird. I've touched alien code. I've battled the AI. I realize Red Kite is actually right—I am dangerous. The only question is who is in the greatest danger from my being alive—the AI, the Rogues, or me?

# Chapter Ten

*You can be heard. All you have to do is challenge the leaders for the right.*

Bird's words echo in my mind. It seems odd she'd tell me something like this—we haven't always been friends, and she hated the biogear I had the Tracker Clan using. Is this more about her supporting Wolf and the Tracker Clan against the other clans? And do I really want to tell my whole story to all these strangers?

I'm not sure about that, and since we've lost the tunnels, I'm not sure Bird has her smoke to see visions any longer. But Bird and I at least came to terms about not using biogear—it was making me too much like the AI. Does Bird now think I can save the Rogues—and the world—from the AI? Or does she still see doom ahead for all of us, just as the AI showed me? Maybe she thinks it doesn't matter what anyone says—that it's action that matters. I'd have to agree with that idea. But do I do as she's urging and challenge the clan leaders? Is that really going to get anything done?

With a soft groan, I roll over. I'm tired…so very tired. The Glass Hall never seems to grow darker or lighter—it just is. And while my fingers itch to get back to the room that must be Dr. Sig's lab, I should wait until I'm rested. Going there exhausted isn't going to help me uncover new data, and I want to be cautious about dealing with the alien code. I don't know if that's what's really wrong with the AI, or if that could be our salvation.

I've found an empty corner of the hall. It is warm enough to use my outer shirt and my pouch for a pillow. Oddly, the floor seems soft—softer than dirt or sand—even though it seems to be glass. It's warm and my mind starts to drift into odd dreams.

*The Glass Hall is empty. Panic races through me in a sharp bite like that of the biogear connecting, but I don't know why. My heart hammers against my chest. I have no idea where everyone has gone.*

*"Skye?" I call out, but I don't. That is the way of dreams, but I can't seem to wake myself. My voice echoes against the hard walls.*

*Something on the floor flutters ...a brightly colored ribbon. It is from Bird. She wears ribbons pinned to her skin clothing and in her hair.*

*With trembling fingers, I pick up the ribbon. "Bird? Where are you?"*

*This is just a dream, but it feels so real. I hear a laugh behind me and spin around. Nothing.*

*The laugh, low and taunting, echoes again from behind me. This time when I turn, I glimpse a shadow.*

*I follow it, heading back to Dr. Sig's lab. Inside the room, the shadow seems to be lurking, hiding in the walls, but how can it do that.*

*Gripping the ribbon tightly as if that will anchor me, I grind out the question. "What is going on?"*

*A soft voice answers me. "Lib."*

*I turn again, expecting another shadow, but this time Constance Sig stands in her lab. Or is this the AI who wears Dr. Sig's face? Is there even a difference between them?*

*I study the features I know so well—brown hair pulled up and back. Her hair lays perfectly smooth. Her face is oval with a chin that tapers to a point. The high cheekbones and hollows below and the sharp jaw line make her seem angular. Her body is angular as well—tall and lean. Like me. I cannot tell if her eyes are those of the AI— are they too blue? Too bright? Or am I dreaming of Dr. Sig? She steps closer to me. "I've been waiting for you to find me, Lib."*

*Now I am confused. I take a step backwards. My back hits a glass wall. For a moment, I feel as if I am staring at my own reflection in glass, not at Dr. Sig. But I am not her. Shaking my head, I tell her, "I've been searching for Dr. Sig."*

*Is that true? Is that why I keep going back to the Empties?*

*Her smile widens. "Have you been trying to come home?"*

*It sounds so nice—home. I have a home with the Tracker Clan, but we lost our tunnels. Do we live here now?*

*As if she knows my thoughts—and why wouldn't she if she is part of my dream—she gestures to the Glass Hall. "Home."*

*I glance around the room—the lab. It looks different today. The walls display screens, all of them humming with energy. A soft, lavender glow seems to be emanating from them. This is the mix of alien gear and what Dr. Sig created—this is how it should be.*

*"This is where it started, don't you remember?"*

*I frown. "Why would I remember? I wasn't here."*

*"But you were. I was here. This is where we fused two technologies to create the future." Turning, she walks to a wall and touches a screen. Code dances over the screen—I know it, and yet I don't.*

*And now I don't know if I am dreaming, or if I have connected to the Glass Hall somehow. Is this really Dr. Sig? Have I found her?*

*She turns to face me. "And now you know what you have to do, don't you?"*

*Her eyes seem to glow brighter—and bluer. Is this really Dr. Sig—or Conie, the AI? Conie—Control Over the Normal Inhabited Environment. The AI created to monitor and maintain the Norm. But now the AI wants to take the Norm away from this world and destroy everything left behind.*

*"It's the only way," she says in that same calm voice. A dream voice. "We have to save the Earth. It's time—"*

I jerk awake and sit up. That either breaks the dream or breaks my connect to whatever lives within the walls of the Glass Hall. Sweat sticks my skin shirt to my back and drips down between my breasts. I'm breathing hard and shaking. I wipe at the sweat cooling on my face, blink and try to focus on the main hall. Hot panic sears through me—I can't see any of the Rogue clans. Why aren't they here?

A hand clamps down on my shoulder. "You're up. Good."

Alis offers me a water skin and sits beside me. "You slept really late, but I figured it didn't matter."

"Where is everyone?"

She waves a hand to the entrance of the Glass Hall. "Out on scavenges. Seems most of the other clans scavenge by day—or at least the Fighter Clan does and they pretty much either shamed or strong-armed the other clans into going out with them. Said we need supplies and food and Red Kite said she knows where to get both."

Rubbing my eyes, I glance around. I still do not know if that was a dream, a vision, or a connect. I glance at the floor, and decide it would be best not to touch it with my bare hands.

Alis digs into the pouch hanging across her chest and pulls out a chunk of dried meat. "Hungry?"

With a nod, I take the meat and take a bite. It's dried snake, salty, but good. I end up eating the rest of it quickly, take a long drink of water and then ask, "Where's Skye? Did she go with the others? And where are those who were hurt? They can't be out on a scavenge."

Alis waves to an area on our right. "Croc set up a room for the injured. He's with them now. Skye went exploring. She said she didn't want to sit around doing nothing, and she didn't want to hang around a bunch of Rogues who can't figure the truth when it's shoved under their noses." Her mouth twists up on one side. "I happen to agree with her so I stayed."

I offer her a faint smile and nod. But now I am worried.

80

The AI has connected to me before in dreams. I had thought the Glass Hall might be safe from Conie—but is it?

Alis clears her throat and nudges my arm with her elbow. I glance at her. I realize she has gotten some of the dust off her face and hair. She wears her red hair pulled back now.

"Did you find a bath?" I ask. I miss the hot springs from our old tunnels.

She shakes her head. "Water is too precious here to waste on bathing, but one of the Hills Clan gave me a cloth she scavenged and it got most of the dust off me." She glances away, and then looks back and says, "I heard what Bird told you yesterday. About telling your story to the clans. Are you going to do it? Do you think it'll help?"

My stomach churns and I put a hand over it and press down. "What do you think?"

She lifts a hand and pulls a face, and then looks away. Scooting over, she props her back against the wall. Alis is not the type to show her emotions, but I see a touch of hope in her eyes.

Looking away, I shake my head. "No, I'm not going to try to speak to the clans again. They won't listen, and…and telling them everything I know is not a good idea."

She tugs at a loose bit of thread that holds her skin pants together. "Why not?"

I take another drink of water to give myself time to order my words. "The clans will either help or not. Wolf will convince them—or not. My story…I've told them what they need to know. Now they have to make their own choices. We all do."

And that's what this is coming down to—choices to make.

*     *     *

The Rogue clans come back with very little to show from the scavenge. I notice the other clans giving Red Kite dirty looks, as if they now doubt her words. If she said she knew of a good place to scavenge, she has failed. That's not a good thing in a leader.

Wolf heads over to me. I've been pacing in the Glass Hall, torn between the desire to go back to Dr. Sig's lab and worried about the dream—or whatever it was. I can't risk a connect if I cannot control the hack. Skye is back from exploring, and she and the others from the Tracker Clan are gathered to divide up the few bits of plant roots from the scavenge.

Wolf grabs my arm and leads me to a place in the Glass Hall behind one of the glass walls. Everyone can still see us, but they won't be able to hear whatever Wolf has to say.

"How did the scavenge go?" It is a stupid thing to ask—I can see the meager results—but I want to get Wolf talking.

He gives a low growl and slashes a hand in the air as if knocking away the question. "Bird told me she urged you to challenge the clan leaders. I think she's right. I think most will hear you."

I let out a breath and wrap my arms around me. "Do you really think they want to hear how I can make connects that no one else can? That I look like Dr. Sig—like the AI? Do they want to hear I can...I can make hacks here in the Glass Hall, and I'm not sure I should be able to do that. I'm not even sure I am trustworthy."

His dark eyes narrow. "Lib, hacks are what you do. Special does not mean bad."

I take a breath and tell him of my dream. And how I don't know if it really was Dr. Sig—a connect to her here in this place—or if the AI can connect to me.. "If the AI—if Conie—can reach me in here, that means I'm a danger to every Rogue." I wave my arms around us. "This is what she wants—all the Rogues, or almost all of them, and the Glitches in one place."

Wolf stares at me. He shakes his head and stands straighter. "You fought the AI. You have gone into the Norm to the AI. You are not the AI."

"I have things I don't remember about myself—things I don't trust in myself." I shake my head. "What if I'm giving everyone the wrong information? The AI said she made me—she made with a blend of biology and gear and the AI put Dr. Sig's DNA inside me. I don't know how much of Dr. Sig I have—do I have her memories, or just her mind and her face? Or am I really a lot more like the AI? Is that why it was so easy for me to use the biogear—because that's what I am? Part machine? Is that really what you want me to tell the Rogue clans?"

His expression softens and he steps closer. He puts his hands on my shoulders. "You are not a drone or a scab. You are Lib. You know the AI because you can connect with it—that is our advantage. That is the reason why we can fight. You are not tainted—you are gifted and we need your gifts, Lib."

I search his eyes—I want to believe him. I want to trust that he is right.

*But what if I am the one built wrong?*

The thought tugs on me, leaving me even more worried.

I open my mouth, wanting to argue with him—wanting him to keep reassuring me.

The shaking ground stops my words and leaves me staring.

At first I wonder if I'm the one quivering. But Wolf glances up and says, "Earth's moving again."

The glass walls rattle. Everything seems to sway. Wolf wraps his arms around me and pulls me close as if to shield me. He backs us up until we're next to a wall, but I'm not sure that will provide any protection. I keep thinking of the tunnels collapsing, of how the tower in the Empties—the other Empties—fell. The glass around us flexes and wobbles as though made of water. Shouts echo through the rooms. Many of the Rogues stagger and run to get outside. I can't move. Others do like Wolf and find a spot to stand against what seem to be the outside walls. I hope the other Trackers are safe—that Croc has the injured tucked into corners and that Alis and Skye have found a spot to ride this out, and that Bird is okay.

Wolf holds me tightly, sheltering me with his body. I cling to him, an urgent thought racing through my mind.

*This cannot last.*

I'm right. The shaking gets worse and the glass walls warp and shift and shatter.

# Chapter Eleven

The shaking stops at last, leaving behind an eerie silence. I am shivering now, but still in Wolf's arms and still on my feet. He shifts, and I do as well and glance around.

No one seems to be injured—at least I don't see blood or bodies sprawled on the floor like dead animals. Everyone is still on their feet. I count clans—Tracker, Hills, Sing-Song, Walking Tall. I see only a few red-clay painted faces of those in the Fighter Clan. Most of them fled outside. They will have a hard time living down the fact they did not stand with the other clans.

Wolf lets go and heads out to help the others. I follow him. First thing we check on is Croc and the injured. The room Croc chose went through the shaking better than the main hall. Everyone there is well and no glass has fallen. Wolf asks Bird to help Croc mend any cuts or bruises, but Croc snaps back that what he needs are the healing herbs and better supplies. We all need water. I can see we will have to do another scavenge soon. But not now.

All the clans work to clear the broken glass. That is harder than dealing with it falling, and a few end up with cut hands. Everyone speaks in low tones, and shares nervous glances to check the walls and ceilings and make sure they are not going to fall on us.

The Glass Hall no longer seems to be the safe place. But where else can we go?

Alis comes over to me and asks, "What do you think they're talking about?" She nods to the Fighting Clan who are clustered in one corner and talking with each other.

I shrug. "Probably about the ground shaking."

She gives me a sideways look and says, "Maybe now is the time to tell them your story. Maybe they'll listen."

Skye comes over and asks, "Who'll listen to what?"

Alis opens her mouth to answer. Before she can, I tell Skye, "Nothing. It's not important."

Shaking her head, Alis says, "It is important. You've said so yourself. We have to stop the AI and destroy the Norm and we can't do that without all the Rogues helping."

Skye stiffens and turns to face Alis. "The Norm isn't such a terrible place, you know that. You've been there—you were once a Tech, too." She turns and walks away, her hair swinging.

Crow comes over to where Alis and I stand and asks, "What was that about?"

I shake my head, but I tell him, "The Norm was Skye's home—and…and she's right. It can be nice in the Norm. They have green plants—grass and trees. And food and water, and it's never too hot or cold." I let out a long breath "In some ways it's perfect. So long as you do what the AI wants you to do."

"And don't glitch up a program," Alis said, her voice bitter. "You glitch the work—the AI throws you out like trash. That's why the AI has to go." She walks away, heading the opposite direction from the path Skye took.

Crow watches her and then glances at me. "But it's not for you, right? It's not your home. You're clan now."

He stares at me as if looking for something in my face that will confirm his words. I part my lips to tell him something…but the truth is, I'm not sure what to answer.

Yes, I'm clan. I joined the Rogues. But we've lost our home in the tunnels. My memories are fragments, and what I have pieced together all seems linked to the AI. And to Dr. Constance Sig.

Letting out a breath, I tell Crow, "Maybe…maybe I am more of a Rogue than anything else, but right now all I seem to have are questions. I don't know what to tell you."

Crow touches the back of my hand with one finger. "You're clan. That's all you need to know."

I wish that was true.

Crow glances around us. "It won't be safe to stay here." His voice is cool, almost icy. I wonder if he is thinking of those in the Tracker Clan buried in the tunnels.

But I also know I cannot leave this place. There are answers here that I need. I glance around us. "It doesn't matter if this place is safe or not—very soon, nowhere on this world will be safe." I turn to look at Crow and focus my attention on him. "We can't hide. We can't run. The AI intends to crack this world open and destroy everything. Nothing will survive."

Turning, I walk away and start to make my way back to the lab. I need answers. Alis wants me to talk to all the clans, but I don't want to do that when I still have questions. And Skye's words leave me wondering if it is possible to keep the Norm without the AI. I don't think we can—but I need to find out.

# Chapter Twelve

A soft humming echoes through the glass halls. The sound is beautiful. It's also sad and lonely. It's so soft you could almost miss it, but in the hallway to the lab I can hear it echoing against the glass walls. I pause to listen, wondering if this is someone's voice or am I hearing the AI again? The voice sounds familiar, so I follow it.

My steps echo from the hard walls and ceiling. I turn left and right, following the hum, which is so pretty that I am certain it can't be the AI. The sound leads me toward the lab, and I was going there anyway. Is this Skye making this hum? This pretty sound? The walls here have cracks in them now. I touch one. The crack slowly mends itself. Jerking my hand away, I focus on my steps. As I get closer to the lab, I see fewer cracks—it is as if the Glass Hall knows how to heal itself. Which is an odd idea. It is almost as if the place is alive. Is the hall humming?

The sound grows louder, lifts up and then drops down again. It leads me to the entrance to the lab. Inside, Bird wanders the lab, her arms crossed so she is not touching anything. Oddly, the colors in the glass change with her voice as she hums higher and then lower pitches. It is almost as if the walls are echoing Bird's voice, but how can they do that and why would they?

I stand for a moment, listening to her voice, wondering where she learned to make her voice seem so sweet, and wishing I knew how to do this. She seems to become aware of me for her voice trails off. She turns and stares at me.

She seems smaller than usual in the lab—the size of the room is bigger than I remember. Bird pushes her hair and ribbons back from her face.

Waving a hand behind me, I tell her, "I'll just go. I didn't mean to interrupt or stop your...your voice."

"No, stay. We should talk."

I almost wish I hadn't followed her voice—I'm not certain I am up to another talk. Alis isn't happy with me and neither is Skye. Is Bird going to tell me, too, that I need to talk to the clan?

But there's something gentle about her words and tone. I think back to when Skye first brought me to the Tracker Clan and Bird was the one to talk Wolf into letting me be part of the clan. She once trusted me and convinced Wolf to give me a chance. But that was before she started to have visions about me—and before I started to have dreams of death.

Stepping into the lab, I glance around. The glass walls turn a pale white now. What will happen when I touch the walls again? Will the screens appear again? What is it that I can connect to here? My fingers almost itch with the desire to make a connect, but I'm also worried about it enough that I don't mind putting it off for a time.

Bird sits on the floor, legs crossed in front of her as if we are in the tunnels and have a fire in the middle of the room for warmth. She pats the floor, not with invitation to sit, but as if testing it. "Did you notice it's soft? Soft and warm. It's almost like it's been wanting company and is trying to make us welcome."

I shrug and have no idea what to answer. This is just a place. So I tell her, "That was pretty—what you were doing with your voice."

She nods. "It's a song. Not like one from the Sing-Song Clan. They use chants mostly. But my mother used to sing to me when I was little." She frowns and pulls at the ribbons in her hair.

I wander around the room, and come back and sit across from Bird so I can face her. "Your mother was in the See Far Clan—they're not here with the other clans. Crow told me they're gone."

Bird nods. She glanced down at her hands. I wait to see what she might tell me. She was the one who said she wants to talk.

After a long time, Bird says, "I hate them."

"Your old clan?"

She shakes her head, her wild hair bouncing with the movement and the ribbons swaying. "The Fighter Clan. They're why the See Far Clan is gone." She closes her eyes and opens them again. Her eyes seem very bright. "Seeing doesn't always mean you can stop what's coming. But you know that. They're never going to help us—Red Kite will never let them."

Leaning forward to rest my elbows on my thighs, I ask, "Why don't the clans work together? They're all Rogues."

Bird gives a snort. "When you don't have much, you have to fight for what you do have. Clans fight for territory, for water, for…well, for just about any reason. My mother had the vision of the clan dead. She sent me away before it happened. She told me there was no way to stop what was going to happen"

Frowning, I ask, "Why are you telling me this? Do you think all visions are…are locked?"

She tips her head to one side and stares at me. She seems to be considering her answer. She takes a minute as if thinking over what she wants to say. "Because you need to know things. Visions aren't—they aren't always clear. But my mother taught me, just as her mother taught her, that visions are real. Visions are about choices. Do we listen or not? Do we pay attention to warning signs?"

"Why didn't your clan just move if they knew the Fighter Clan was coming to…well, to fight?"

Bird's mouth pulls down and she stares at me as if I've just said something stupid. "And what if by moving that's when the Fighter Clan finds us? Or what if we move right into a trap? A vision can push you into the wrong choice. That's what happened to the See Far Clan. Most thought the clan would be safe if we stayed put. But that was the wrong choice."

I nod and stare down at the floor. It is soft—and warm. I trace a hand over the glass and press my finger into it, and then I look up at Bird. "You think we'll make the wrong choice now? You think hiding, staying put is the wrong choice? Am I going to be the one who pushes the clans into that choice?" She shakes her head, but she doesn't answer me, so I ask, "Your visions told you to tell me all of this?"

She shrugs. "Maybe. I have to make choices, too. And I've run out of smoke, so I'm not even sure I'm going to get any more visions."

Frowning, I ask, "You once said you saw me in shadows—and in ruins. You said I would do great things—and that I bring destruction. You said I'd change the world."

Bird nods. "And I still see a tie between you and our enemy— the AI. That is the shadow—and it grows stronger. Larger. It will swallow you one day."

I shake my head. "I thought you said we had choices—that visions showed choices. I have a choice about that. I have no intent to let the AI swallow me."

Bird pushes up to her feet in one smooth movement. "The visions aren't all that clear sometimes. Just whispers in the dark. But take the warning. The Rogues won't follow you—not all of them. You get the Fighter Clan on your side, you'll lose the Tracker Clan and the Walking Tall Clan. The Hills Clan won't follow anyone, and the Sing-Song Clan can't fight worth anything. You're going to have to make choices about who follows you—and who dies because of that." She doesn't sound angry—just resigned. She waves an arm around her. "Stay. Find what you need."

With her ribbons fluttering, she walks out of the lab.

Standing, I put a hand on my hip and think about going after Bird to ask about her vision—what might be her last vision. But if it wasn't that clear, what else would she be able to tell me. And do I even want to know more? Bird is right—visions are a two-edge blade. A vision can push you into doing the wrong thing at the wrong time. The See Far Clan would have done better to have guards posted instead of relying on some blurry sight of what might happen.

But still...is Bird right? What if I am destined to be swallowed by the AI?

Conie wanted that, the last time I confronted her—the last time I tried to destroy her with Raj's virus code. She went from using me, to trying to destroy me, to wanting me integrated with her because of all I have learned. But that is not going to happen.

Shaking my head, I face the lab—Dr. Sig's lab.

*Stay. Find what you need.*

"What I need?" I murmur. Well, at least Bird is pointing me to do something I already plan to do.

I walk around the room slowly, staring at the walls. For a moment, it seems to me I still hear Bird's...song. Her humming. But this is not Bird's voice, and this is not the high and low hum of Bird's song. This is a low, steady hum. It sounds more like the whirring of a drone.

Frowning, I try to follow the sound. The humming seems to be stronger from only one section of glass wall. When I move away,

I cannot hear the hum, so I head back to the far wall and stand staring at it.

The sound is so soft that it is impossible to hear unless I stand in front of the wall. The hum vibrates within my chest. I step closer and touch the wall.

A screen appears. I place my palm on it. My fingers tingle.

*I must find what I need—and I need answers.*

For a moment, the screen brightens. A light moves from the top of the screen downward, over my hand. My fingers tingle once more. And then a new doorway opens—the glass turns from white to transparent and slides back. I pull my hand from the screen and poke my head into the doorway.

The room beyond is small—much smaller than the lab. I step inside and turn in a slow circle, trying to take in everything. The walls do not seem to be glass, but look like brushed metal of some kind with panels inset into the walls. Light glitters along tubes that connect the panels. Looking up, the ceiling seems to be a copy of the night sky for I see stars—thousands of them— against the black ceiling.

Is this another lab—a hidden one? I'm not sure. The humming is louder in this room, as if the walls are really machines—as if I am inside a drone or something else. I do not know if this is more alien tech or something Dr. Sig or someone else created. I listen for a moment, and hear the humming coming from my left.

Turning, I walk over to the panel that is to my left. A bright light blinks on and off, like the flickering of a fire in a strong wind. Why is there power here? Why is the Glass Hall different from anything else in the Empties—in any of the Empties?

I reach out to the panel, but hesitate. Pulling my hand back, I rub my palm over the leg of my trousers. The skins I wear—tanned and thin—give me no comfort. Do I really want to do this? Touching this will make a connect—but to what?

Now Bird's warning sits heavy in my stomach and on my chest. This could connect to the AI—this could be a trap. Or this could connect to information that I must have to answer my questions. I think about the See Far Clan and their choice to stay put—it did not help them. The same thing will happen to us. If we stay put here in the Glass Hall the world will continue to shake apart—until we are no more. I have no real choice here.

Taking a breath, I lay my palm flat against the panel. A familiar tingling spreads over my fingers and into my hand.

*Connection: Secure.*

With a blink, I seem to be in blackness. This is not the cool blue of the AI's artificial world—this is something else. The black reminds me of the ceiling in this room, and the hum is a soft noise that seems comforting. Color begins to spark into existence around me, tiny spots of white that look like the embers from a fire lit with wood that holds a great deal of sap. Yellows and soft blues swirl around me and into amazing shapes that are unlike anything I've seen before.

I almost feel weightless, as if I am floating amid stars. My skin feels warm, as if I am bathed in light, but I have no idea where I am.

This is not the AI's virtual world, but it is a connect and so it should have the same rules.

I reach out with my mind to summon a screen just like I would within the AI's world. It appears—but what should I search for? Frowning, I try to think of all the questions I have.

Symbols and lines of code flashing over the screen blur together. I want to slow them down or stop them. Somehow, I know this code, but I *shouldn't*. I have no memory of learning this. I want to shout at it to stop—to give me what I want, but I still have no questions to ask that could change the display.

And then suddenly the code vanishes and a face appears—but it is Conie or Dr. Sig staring at me now?

# Chapter Thirteen

For a moment, my heart thuds fast and heavy, beating against my ribs in a way that makes my head spin. I suck in a sharp breath and hold it, my chest tight. I know Conie's eyes—the too-blue eyes of the AI that are impossible on any living person. This woman does not have those eyes. Her eyes seem pale and she also does not really seem to be seeing me. She glances around her as if checking to see if anyone is near. Behind her, I can see the glass walls of this lab. When she faces forward again, she starts to talk, and I realize this is Dr. Sig. Or it was—this is a message she left here somehow with abilities we no longer really have.

"Day nine-hundred-sixty-two of the Normandy Project. We're experiencing some minor setbacks regarding the virtual construction. Integration initially went relatively smooth, but minor glitches have arisen in terms of expected power usage."

Reaching out, I touch her face. Glitches—she uses the word to mean a problem, but that is not what a Glitch is here in this world. She does not react to my touch but keeps talking, her voice dry, as if nothing is wrong, as if she is not in the process of creating something that now wants to destroy this world. She purses her lips and lines form along the edges of her mouth. With her high, sharp cheekbones, the lines make her look older. She lets out a breath and begins speaking again. "The alien technology is primarily organic in composition and as a result is not adapting to the power supplies we've been trying to use. Solar and wind power seems to work well, but we need to set up some other source—possibly geothermal—due to the demands put on the system." She pauses, rubs at the lines on her forehead and begins to speak faster. "The time frame doesn't allow for errors. We need a permanent barrier of protection over cities that can sustain itself. If we fail, everyone is at risk from the unstable climate we've created. Dr. Regis thinks it's a mistake to alter the organic imprinting within the alien technology, but I can't see any other choice. Organic technology means a system that can regenerate and repair itself. It's going to need power, and it will need stasis periods—much like sleep for the human body. But the real trick is going to be the energy to sustain its own artificial body—the environment we're creating."

She stops again. I struggle to understand her. Some of it makes sense. Normandy—is that the Norm? She must be speaking of the AI—it is the only thing I know that has alien technology, and she says it is organic, like a body. That makes sense. The drones and scabs made by the AI have organic components. I may also be something like that. But it is hard to think of the Norm as a massive body for the AI. However, this starts to make sense. The AI needs water and fuel—or rather the Norm needs these things. But how is any of this information going to help bring down the AI?

On the recording, Dr. Sig flashes a tight smile as if she is not really happy with her own thoughts. "We may have to take bigger risks with the integration. I don't see any choice about that, either"

Choices. Did she make the wrong choice in creating the AI? From how she speaks, she sounds as if the world was in worse shape during her time than it is now. I find that difficult to believe. How could it have been worse than our brutal sun during the day and our cold nights? But I've had dreams of terrible floods. Is that what happened? Did they somehow make the world's weather go wrong, and it is only now correcting itself? Or is the AI tampering with the climate as well? I know it can.

Dr. Sig's voice drops to a low tone as if she doesn't want anyone to hear her words. "We are too close to stop. There is too much at stake. I'm—"

Her words cut off and her image vanishes, leaving the screen blank. A sharp jolt runs through me, stabbing up from my palm. With a gasp, I jerk away.

Swaying, I glance around. I am back in the room near Dr. Sig's lab and no longer in the virtual world within the Glass Hall.

I stare at the panel, my hands shaking and my breaths coming in short gasps. I've been disconnected.

The Glass Hall threw me out.

That's never happened to me. I've influenced other connects, and I've pulled Skye and others from connects gone bad, so I know it's possible to sever a link like that. But this was as if the Glass Hall itself pushed me out.

Why did it do that?

Frowning, I brace my back and put my hand on the panel again. Nothing happens. The glass under my hand remains cool, as if it is no longer active. Given how old everything must be, it really is not much of a surprise—the power must be fading here.

Unless Dr. Sig found a way to that power source she spoke of—geothermal. It must be power from the ground.

Pulling my hand away, I rub my face, and realize this is the same gesture I saw Dr. Sig make. With a shiver, I turn away and head out of the lab. I don't want to think about how I seem to becoming more and more connected to Dr. Sig.

I'm hungry and tired—and an idea is swirling around in my head that I don't really like.

What if there is more inside me than just Dr. Sig's DNA? What if the AI gave me some of her memories and her knowledge? That would explain why I know things without any idea of how I learned them. But does that mean I will make the same mistakes Dr. Sig made in creating the AI?

***

Back in the Glass Hall, the clans are meeting again, and I hear mutters, questions about if it is safe to stay here or not. The leaders of the clan sit separate from the others, but the Tracker Clan is easy to spot, grouped around what once was a wall. They pass around dried meat and skins of water that look a little too thin. I go to sit with them. The dried meat is tough, but filling. I eat a little bit and watch as Wolf sits with his shoulders hunched and listens to the other clan leaders.

I've become familiar enough with the clans to identify them easily, but what matters more is who seems to be supporting Wolf and the Tracker Clan and who is not.

It does seem as if the Walking Tall Clan is on Wolf's side. A few of their clan mingle with the Tracker Clan, sharing water, and their clan leader, Mountain, sits next to Wolf. He is well named for he is big and bulky, huge as a mountain. The Fighter Clan still worries me. They all sit hunched over, their bodies tense as if they are hoping a fight will break out. They look eager to leave for they have taken up the space next to the entrance. From what Red Kite is now saying about how a clan should look after its own, I don't think we're going to get any support from them.

*Why are they even here?*

Glancing around, I search for Alis and Skye, but they are not in the hall. They must be out on a scavenge. Crow and Bird are also missing, which means they're out as well. Frowning, I wonder now how long did that connect in Dr. Sig's lab last? It did not seem more than moments, but now I begin to think I was there for far longer than I knew. That's why I came out hungry and tired—I was lost in the Glass Hall's virtual world.

That thought chills my skin. Maybe it was a good thing it threw me out.

Unwilling to dwell on the idea that I might never have disconnected if the Glass Hall had not dropped me out, I try to listen to what the clans are saying. But the meeting seems to have ended. Red Kite and the Fighter Clan are heading outside. Red

Kite turns back to Wolf and she says something about the night sky being safer than glass.

Wolf just shakes his head and turns away from her. His glance sweeps the room and then finds me. His dark eyes look worried. He heads to my side and sits down, his knees bent and his arms resting on them. He looks tired, his eyes seem a little dull and his shoulders sag as if he has come back from a bad scavenge.

"Wolf?" I just say the one word, leaving the question hanging. Does he need something from me? Something other than me talking to the clans again?

He glances at me and says, "The shaking did more than break glass—it shook the clans, or some of them. Walking Tall Clan is with us, but the others can't decide what to do. Fighter Clan wants to go back to their own territory—or some of them do. Some of them want a fight." He glances at me and his mouth curves. "Missed you. Been exploring?"

I nod and offer back a small smile. I also reach up to touch his face. I need to touch something real—something that is a connect to a warm body and not to cold virtual worlds that leave me confused. He doesn't move as I touch him. His face is rough with his beard, and I wonder if he worries about what the other clans think to see a clan leader with a Glitch—a former Tech. I know Red Kite thinks little of me—probably the others do, too. The other clans have no Glitches with them, which tells me a lot about how they don't really take in anyone who gets thrown out of the Norm.

*I know you care…I do, too.*

I try to send Wolf those thoughts. His eyes warm as if he understands. I pull my hand away, but he touches a fingertip to my cheek, echoing the move I made. His touch leaves my skin tingling, me and the way his gaze lingers sends a jolt into my stomach that settles even lower inside me.

"You were gone a long time," Wolf says.

I bite my lower lip and then ask, "How long?"

"Two meals. If you'd missed this one I was going to have to track you down."

"Here?" I glance around at all the glass. "No footprints, no traces. The Glass Hall is really a maze of halls and rooms." Looking away, I pull in a breath, let it out and tell him, "I spoke to Bird. She still worries I'm connected to the AI and will be even more so. I worry, too. So I went looking for answers."

"Did you find what you need?"

The way his words echo Bird's forces my stare up to his eyes. I search his face, wondering if he has spoken to Bird, but Wolf just stares back at me, his eyes dark and unreadable. The Glass Hall has put new lines around his eyes and mouth. With a start, I realize he, too, worries this may no longer be safe. Unlike the other clans, the Tracker Clan has no place to go back to. "Would the Walking Tall Clan take us in?"

He shrugs. "Maybe. They'll consider it. Maybe not. The ground shook again while you were gone."

I lick my lips. More shaking—but I felt nothing while I was in the Glass Hall's virtual world. Does that mean I was elsewhere?

Glancing around at the Rogues, a plan starts to form—something Dr. Sig said starts to make more sense. The Norm is the AI's body. We've been trying to attack the AI's mind—to strike at the AI's core. But what if we could do just as much damage by striking at the AI's body—at the Norm. That's a target the Rogues might understand. It's real and the dome is something everyone can see.

I look over at Wolf. "I think I have an idea—but we're going to need more than the help of just one clan."

Wolf nods. "What's your thinking?"

I shake my head. "Would the clans feel better about attacking the Norm? It's…it's metal and protected. But the Rogues understand hitting back against drones and scabs—those are real, too. The AI…it's more like a concept. It's not real, not like the shaking. And if they understand that's coming from the Norm—"

"They'd strike back." Wolf sits up a little straighter. "It's a good idea."

Swallowing the dryness in my mouth, I ask, "Do you think I need to talk to the clans?"

He shakes his head, pats my hand and stands. "No. Let me sound out the others first. I've heard stories of the Sing-Song Clan—that they have things that make the Fighter Clan think twice about attacking them. And the Walking Tall Clan is said to have been the first to scavenge the Empties. Mountain once told me he'd found weapons that can bring down drones. I thought he was just boasting. We have to make certain of them."

I nod. Wolf looks a little less tired now. He leaves me to seek out the other clan leaders—or at least to seek out Mountain and Iguana. I scoot back until I can lean against a wall, and start to think of a plan that will not be pure suicide for everyone.

Attacking the Norm is going to wake the AI and Conie will send out every done and scab she has to fight back against us.

*       *       *

Crow, Alis, Skye and Bird come back empty-handed from their scavenge. Alis and Skye head over to me, both of them dusty and their hair tugged and twisted. Outside the Glass Hall, I can hear the low moan of the wind. Alis spits out sand. "Storm coming."

Skye nods and tries to brush the dirt from her hair, which is now the same color as the sand. "Just beat it back here. Couldn't find a platform that worked."

"Couldn't find anything," Alis mutters. "Animals knew sand was starting to blow and headed underground."

Glancing at her and frowning, Skye says, "Bird got Croc some of the herbs he's been wanting—that's something."

Alis grumbles about how herbs won't help us with not having much water left. I agree, and I start to wonder if I can make a connect here, could I find water as well as power?

However, water really is the least of my worries right now.

The plan I've been forming is dangerous—one that could leave every Rogue here dead. I know the AI has far more drones than the Rogues could ever defeat. But I have an idea about that, as well. One that is going to fulfill Bird's prophecy—and that frightens me.

To get my mind off my worries, I help Alis and Skye shake the sand from their clothes. From across the hall, Crow gives me a nod, but he doesn't come over to talk. Wolf is still meeting with the other clans. Now Wolfe has not just Mountain, leader of the Walking Tall Clan, with him, but Faun of the Sing-Song Clan is listening to them, as is Iguana of the Hills Clan. That must be a good sign. Alis and Skye settle back to sip water, eat a little dried meat and talk about the scavenge. I listen with only part of my attention. Across the Glass Hall, Red Kite and the others in the Fighter Clan have come back inside to escape the wind and sand. Red Kite steps up to Crow. She stands with her feet apart and one hand on her knife hilt—but that's how she usually sands. She doesn't smile, but she also doesn't look braced and ready to fight. Crow doesn't move away, but turns toward her as if he doesn't really like her being at his back. He folds his arms across his chest, and his mouth tugs down in a harsh frown. The scar that cuts the side of his face seems pale against his tanned skin.

I can't make out what they're saying, but Crow is rigid, unmoving. His jaw is clenched and he digs his fingers into his arms, creasing the skins of the dusty coat he wears. Red Kite steps closer and drops her hand from her knife to her side. She actually gives a small smile. It's odd to see her being anything but aggressive. She keeps her voice low and gestures almost as if inviting Crow to come and sit with her and with the Fighter Clan.

I wonder if Crow still has family or friends with his old clan? If he does, he doesn't seem interested in Red Kite's invitation for he shakes his head and takes a deliberate step back. He says something that leaves Red Kite frowning. She turns away, but glances back at Crow over her shoulder. She gives a single, decisive nod and leaves Crow standing on his own.

Crow does not move, but watches Red Kite walk away.

Alis and Skye are now talking about trying another scavenge tomorrow, but I cannot stop watching Crow. What did Red Kite say to him? Is she trying to get him to rejoin the Fighter Clan? Crow shakes his head and turns away, but he doesn't come back to the Tracker Clan. Instead, he heads to one of the many hallways in the Glass Hall and disappears into another room.

I wait to see if he will come back. He doesn't. Part of me wants to seek him out and make sure he is not angry—he is my friend. But I keep thinking of his face as he walked out—how tight his expression was and how he looked as if he only wanted peace and solitude. I know what that wish is like, and I like Crow enough to give him the chance to find what he needs, too.

But curiosity keeps tugging at me.

Does Crow still have a connection to his old clan? Could that be useful to Wolf in convincing the Fighter Clan to help? I hate to

109

have to think that way, but my plan means we need all the clans—especially the Fighter Clan. They must know how to battle drones. And they should welcome the kind of fight I'm thinking about.

At last, Wolf breaks away from the other clan leaders. Getting up, I head to his side. I need to hear what he has learned. Do the other clans really have weapons they've been keeping secret?

Wolf meets me in the middle of the Glass Hall and takes my hand. He glances around us, sees others watching and so he takes me with him, down yet another hallway, a different one from that chosen by Crow. However, I change the direction and tug him with me, pulling him with me to Dr. Sig's lab.

Once we are inside the lab, Wolf turns to me. He keeps hold of my hand. His voice is heavy and weary when he says, "Two of the clans will help. But..." He runs a hand through his dark hair. His brows pull together in a frown.

I step up to him and put my hands on his chest. "We're going to take this fight to the AI—to the Norm. You know that. We have to."

"The clans fear the AI—the Norm. But they're becoming even more frightened of the shaking. If you have a plan, they'll listen."

I let out a breath. "Wolf, what I'm thinking about...it could all go wrong. It could be an even faster end to everything than if the AI leaves." He nods and lets go of my hand. But only to wrap his arms around my waist. His hands are warm. He pulls me closer, his hands strong and yet also gentle. "I know. We're out of time. And that means there's no better time."

Leaning down, he puts his mouth on mine.

# Chapter Fourteen

My head whirls as if I'm in a connect and spinning down new lines of a virtual world. Something in my heart eases. Wolf has done this before, but never have I felt him so hungry—as if he wants to devour me.

He walks me backward until my shoulders touch the glass. Smiling a little, I reach up and tangle my fingers in his hair. Sand drifts down. We seem to have sand everywhere these days. Wolf tugs at my shirt, lifting it so he can touch more of me. His skin seems hot against mine.

I don't know what he's thinking, but I'm enjoying the stroke of his fingers over my belly and sides. My heart speeds up and my skin warms. My breaths come quick and shallow. I lick at his lips, wanting to taste more of him, wanting to feel and not think for a change.

He breaks off and pulls back, but rests his forehead against mine. "Join with me. If things do go bad, I want memories of you. I want you. And not just because this might be our last chance, but because I've always wanted you. Even when it hasn't been the smartest thing. You're my match, Lib."

Reaching up, I stroke his face. At times he seems so old— other times, like now, he seems younger than I am. Except I have no real idea how old I am. Maybe I am as old as Dr. Sig—or I am in a way. "Memories. You know, neither of us might survive attacking the Norm."

He looks down at our entwined hands, studying them for a moment, and looks up again. "Some things last. I want to touch your soul, Lib."

"I don't know if I—"

He puts a finger over my lips. "You have one. I know. I wouldn't want you like this if you didn't. Join with me."

He squeezes my hand, and I nod. I am not really certain what he's talking about—this joining. It must be like a connect, and I want that with him. Things are bad, but right now in this moment, they aren't *so* bad.

He pulls off my shirt with one easy move and does the same with his own. Then he pulls me to him so our skin is pressed together. I can feel his heart beating fast. My own echoes the pace. He strokes his hands down my back and I do the same to him, marveling at the hard muscles under my touch. This is what I want—I want him. I want a connect to him.

His fingers stray to my trousers, but I already want them gone. I pull away and drag off my boots and my trousers so I stand before Wolf in nothing but skin. He does the same. His body is harder than my own—muscled, his skin darker, rougher. He has more hair on his arms and legs—for I seem to have none. He puts a hand on the place where my neck joins my shoulder and then runs his hand down to the bumps on my chest. He has muscle there, but when he touches me, peaks rise up and my body stirs in ways it never has before.

"Wolf?" I don't know what I mean with that question, but he puts his mouth on mine again and pulls me down to the floor with him. For a moment, we tangle legs and arms and the floor seems to warm under us and soften. Wolf pulls me up so I straddle his hips. He has more hardness in places where I seem to be nothing but soft wetness.

"Join with me," he says again.

I nod in answer, but I still don't know. A yearning rises in me and falls to low in my belly. An ache starts between my legs and when Wolf puts his hands to my chest and then slides his fingers to my waist, I just say one thing. "Yes."

That seems to be the answer he wants.

His eyes darken. Holding my hips, he lifts me up, seems to guide me, and slips part of him into me. It's like a connect—except there is no prick on my palm. There is only warmth and a little bit of pressure between my legs and then a short stab of pain.

I gasp and close my eyes—that's what you do in a connect. You ride the pain and come out into the virtual world.

But Wolf tells me, "Open your eyes. I want you to see me. I want to see you."

Obeying, I look down at him from where I straddle his hips, part of him pulsing inside me and pulling an answering pulse back. My skin warms and slicks with sweat. This is like when Wolf taught me to fight, but it is also nothing like that. Around me is not the cool blue of the AI's world, or the black of the

Glass Hall's world. Instead, the room seems to warm for us, the walls becoming pale yellow like a sunrise. I touch Wolf's face and he tells me, "Move your hips. Move the way you want. Find what you need."

His words come out strained as if he is holding back. His skin heats and slicks and I lay down to press myself onto him. I wiggle as I do and the slight stab of pain changes into something else—a pressure that makes me want more of Wolf.

Putting my hands either side of his face, I smooth back the hair from his forehead. "Is this a joining? A connect?"

He smiles. "I don't know what a connect's like for you. But this has got to be better."

I give a low hum. He is right—this is better. I move again, wiggling, trying to get more of Wolf into me. I am joined with him—not just with my body, but with my heart and mind and maybe I do have a soul, for something inside me seems to open, seems to expand. For a moment, I close my eyes and see stars— and other things that now seem to have names. Galaxies. Nebula. The words pop into mind—words Dr. Sig knew. Words I know.

Wolf gives a grunt and his hips buck under me. Opening my eyes again, I stare down at him, caught by how beautiful he is. His dark eyes seem to pull me in. I touch his sharp cheekbones, his soft lips, and run my finger down to his chest. He gives another gasp, and says, "Lib, join with me now."

"Aren't we joined?" I ask. But then the heat rushes through me, up into me, spills in like a flow of heat from the sun. It leaves me gasping, breathless, yearning for more and then it is impossible to know what is Wolf's body and what is mine. Grabbing my arms, he pulls me down to put my mouth on his. We are one—we join. His skin is mine, his heat warms my heart, his breath fills my lungs. A cry echoes—his or mine, does not matter. Mine is a cry of joy and of life. I shudder and gasp again, and then I am Lib once more and my body is cooling and wetness slicks my thighs. I shiver, so Wolf pulls me around to lie on my side but also on his body.

I leave my hand on his chest and ask, "This…joining. Do you join with others?"

Wolf smiles and shakes his head. "Some do. Most don't. We might have made a baby just now."

Sitting up, I stare down at him. "What? How?"

He shrugs. "It just happens sometimes after a joining. Your belly will swell and then a small one comes out. Croc knows more about it—and how to stop it."

Frowning, I ask, "Stop it? Why would you stop it?"

Wolf pulls me down again so I am spread over his chest. "Not every clan can feed the mouths it has. And there can be problems—for the baby or the mother."

"Mother," I say, rolling the word around in my mouth. I still have the taste of Wolf on my tongue. "I'm not one now."

"How do you know?" Wolf asks.

I shrug—I just know. My skin cools, but I like the touch of Wolf's skin against mine. "We're going to need all the clans."

116

"Later," he mutters.

Feeling suddenly weary, my body sore and yet feeling as if it is shimmering with light, I let my head fall onto Wolf's broad shoulder. I close my eyes, although I have no intention of sleeping. I'd rather spend these moments with Wolf awake.

But Wolf shifts beneath me. I look up, frowning a little.

He reaches up and cups my cheek, his thumb brushes my skin. "Even the Tracker Clan is divided about what to do."

I shrug. "The Tracker Clan follow you." Even as I say this, I know the truth in the words. And I know I have found what I need.

I need Wolf safe. I need the Tracker Clan to go on. I want a baby with Wolf—I want to join with him again. But that is not a need—not the way that I know I must have him go on in this world. Which means I need to change my plans a little—like Dr. Sig, I must take more risks. I see no other choice.

Wolf closes his eyes and takes a breath, letting it out slowly. His eyes close—he falls asleep easily. But he keeps his arm around me as if even in his sleep he does not want to let go.

# Chapter Fifteen

Beside me, Wolf sleeps. He keeps one arm around me. His breathing is deep and even, and he looks so much younger. His face no longer carries lines of worry and if he dreams, it must be of pleasant things for his mouth curves up slightly.

I envy his sleep, but mine wouldn't be dreamless. And right now I do not want the AI touching my mind—I am still too full of Wolf and our joining.

I'm not really sure what to think of what just happened. My body aches a little, sore in a good way, and my mind is reeling with a thousand different thoughts that are so quick, I can barely understand them myself. Mostly, I feel overwhelmed. I have changed. The joining—Wolf and the joining—have changed me.

Idly, I draw small circles across Wolf's skin, marking the scars he carries from scavenges gone wrong and hunts that were worse. Part of me wants to curl into his side and try for rest, but I slide out from beneath his arm, slow and careful. I want to cry at the loss of his warmth and touch, but I have things to do.

When I'm out from his shelter, I dress in my skin pants, shirt and boots. I have to turn back for one last look at Wolf—all muscle and sinew and bone and strength. He must go on—the Tracker Clan must continue. I must find another plan—or a better way to execute the attack on the Norm.

I head back to the smaller room just off Dr. Sig's lab. I must find out more.

This time I know what I want. I pick out another screen—not the one I used before—and put my palm on it. The humming starts up again, though not as strong as before. It is a reminder that power still exists.

And I can tap into that.

Closing my eyes, I demand a connect. For a moment, nothing happens.

*Diagnostic.*

I give the command. The answer is slow to come, but starts up. The problem is clear at once—the shaking has damaged the glass, breaking connects that bring power. The Glass Hall really is alive—it is one giant system. I can see it now and I shift power, reroute it. The power does come from deep within the ground—much like the energy that once heated the pools of our old tunnels. I can sense the energy and sending it along new glass walls seems easy now.

With a deep breath and my palm tingling, I blink once.

*Connection: Secure.*

I open my eyes to find that same strange blackness and dazzling lights, but this time I know what I'm looking at. The information comes into my mind without my asking. Stars... nebulae...galaxies.

For a moment, I let the screen hum and show me sights no one has seen in perhaps hundreds of years. But this is nothing I need.

I think of the Norm...of the AI...I need to know how it was created if I am to stop it.

My thoughts seem to pull up new information for again, Dr. Sig's face—with her not so blue eyes—appears.

"Day one-thousand-sixty-three of Normandy Project. I'm still having difficulties compensating for the power surges. Every time the program expands, it requires more energy and ultimately we can't process response to the need fast enough." She rubs at her eyes, which are rimmed in red as if she has not slept in far too long. "The self-repair is also not functioning to spec. We'll have to rely on additional outside arms and legs, possibly drones to assist."

The image goes blank, but unlike last time I am still in the darkness of the virtual world. I also have not really learned much, except that the AI and the Norm need the drones. And the AI needs a lot of power.

I need to know more, but I have no means to phrase my requests. Except I keep thinking is there a fundamental flaw within the AI or the Norm?

My questions pulls up another image of Dr. Sig. This time, however, she looks more than tired. Her eyes are shiny and her hair is not pulled back but seems to stick out in small wisps as if she has been puling at it. With a shaky hand, she wipes her nose and inhales deeply and then faces me or faces whatever is recording her message. "Day one-thousand-seventy-two. Dr. Regis had an accident—a malfunction with the main cooling unit. The computer room caught fire. The doors locked before he could get out. I can't be sure, but I think it was deliberate. I think

120

someone—something—didn't want him to get out. However, I'm more worried about the impact of this. We've had budget cuts— and now Dr. N'gouse has put forward an idea that we should simply build one huge spaceship, as if that would be less expensive." Wetness slips down her cheek, leaking from her eyes. She wipes at it and shakes her head. "I don't know if I can do this without Dr. Regis...without Tom."

The image blanks, but now I know something I did not know before—Dr. Sig had been joining with this Dr. Tom Regis. I know because of the look in Dr. Sig's eyes at the end of the recording. I know because of my joining with Wolf—I would look as bad if anything happened to Wolf.

But what did happen? Why was there an accident? Was that the AI that killed Dr. Regis? Or this new person—Dr. N'gouse? And his plan to make a spaceship, is that what influenced the AI to think it could turn the Norm into something that could leave this world?

I am about to think of another question that might get more information when a sharp jolt dances into my palm. It sends me staggering back, breaking the connect—this time I know something is trying to keep me from what I want to find here.

Gritting my teeth, I slap my hand down on the screen—but it remains blank. "I'll find a new one," I mutter. Turning, I search for another screen. I try two more before I get a connect.

*Connection: Secure.*

This time I go searching for whatever is triggering these interrupts. My suspicion is they are timed—too long a connect and something is set to disable the connect. It's a good way to hide information. At least I think that's the case. I have to hope this is something left behind—a safety measure. The AI would be sending in drones by now to stop this, if the AI new this information exists.

It takes longer to tear out what I hope are all the timer traps. I then try to go back and pick up the information from the recorded message left after the last one. Dr. Sig's face comes back on the screen. She looks upset as well as sad, now. Her hair is even a bigger mess, as if she pays no attention to it.

"They won't listen, but biointegration is the only way we're going to solve the power supply issue."

Biointegration? That sounds like biogear—and like the bioengineering the AI's been working on.

*And something I might be.*

She is talking about merging a machine with a living mind. I almost want to reach out and shake her and tell her not to do this—it will end up with a machine that thinks it is alive and knows better than anyone else. This will end up creating the AI—Conie.

But I have no way to reach into the past.

Dr. Sig smiles. She reaches up to something and the image shifts to show the lab behind her. A table rests against one wall with gear of some kind—I've never seen anything that big or complicated. Wires hang off of it and it looks bigger than a person. It's no longer here, so I have no idea what has become of it. Dr. Sig's hand appears and waves at the gear. "I've completed the biocopier with a link to the quantum computer to fully map all neural networks. This should allow all memory engrams to be duplicated in the artificial neural network model with the same pattern reconstructions. The cues to retrieve the engrams should be the same."

I don't know what engrams are, but a network—that I know. It's just things linked. And biocopier sounds like biogear. This must be something that helps her make copies of things—maybe entire people or maybe just their minds.

Dr. Sig steps back so I can see her again. She heads over to her biocopier and presses her palm on it. A screen appears and she does something with it, swipes her fingers over various parts of it. "Initial tests have been positive, but I don't have the time to keep testing—I need results. I need proof this is working and that retrieval is reliable. And that power consumptions can be managed."

"If this goes well, I should be able to create an exact copy of the areas of my mind needed for full functionality of the domes. Once the neural network is complete with the stored engrams, the digital version should be able to continue expanding. This should solve the power issues in that the digital brain will be able to better regulate usage and will function more like a body—taken in nutrients from its surroundings and recycling some materials as well as discarding waste."

She stands in front of her machine and puts her hand onto the screen.

Light flashes, blinding. I have to shield my eyes. The light stutters and fades. Dr. Sig sways as if she is not well, but on the screen of the biocopier is a face I know all too well—it looks like Dr. Sig, but the eyes are too blue.

"A perfectly successful test," Conie says. The AI's voice is stiff and mechanical, not as perfect a copy as it is now. The AI and Dr. Sig stare at each other.

The screen goes black, and I am left staring at nothing. I slip out of the connect and glance around the room, my hands shaking and my heart pounding. Sweat cools on my forehead and I take in a breath.

I've just seen the AI created.

And now I know its weaknesses—it needs power, it has trouble with cooling, and it is unable to make self-repairs, which is why the AI needs drones and scabs, and sentinels inside its virtual world. Dr. Sig thought she'd solved these problems—I'm hoping she didn't.

That may be our only hope.

# Chapter Sixteen

Leaving the lab, I notice Wolf is no longer sleeping in Dr. Sig's lab. His clothes are gone, too. For a moment, my heart tightens. I almost wish he was here, so I could talk to him—or join with him again.

I rub at my eyes and jerk my hand away—I'm copying Dr. Sig's gestures again. I keep thinking about the images I have seen on the recordings. The AI is a copy of Dr. Sig, as am I, it seems. So I am a copy of a copy? Or did the AI make me different? Staring at my hands, I think we must not be exact. The AI would not have been interested in reintegrating me if I was just a copy of it or of Dr. Sig. Somehow I have evolved—changed. Dr. Sig said that would happen—*continue expanding*. Those were her words.

Glancing around the lab, I wonder what happened to her biocopier. It is no longer in the lab. Did someone come and take it away? Was she done with it? Or is it in the Norm now and part of the AI? Somehow, I think the last question is also the right answer. The AI has the biocopier with it in the Norm. How else would the AI be able to make copies of people and minds?

Another thought occurs and I wonder if Raj was copied? Was Raj—the original Raj—killed but his mind was put into a machine? Or into part of the AI? I think this is likely, and it leaves me hating the AI even more.

Heading back to the Glass Hall, my stomach grumbles. I wonder if I've been gone for more than one meal again. I haven't slept. My shoulders sag. My steps drag. I should at least try to get some rest, but my mind keeps spinning.

In the hall, the clans have gathered into small clumps, each clan separate from the others, although it seems to me the Walking Tall Clan sits closer to the Tracker Clan than to anyone else. Perhaps it is a sign of allegiance. The Fighter Clan and the Sing-Song Clan have small fires burning, even though the floors and rooms are warm. Smoke stings my eyes and I give a small cough. Are they cooking a meal, or do they just miss the light from the fire?

I don't see Wolf, but several of the Tracker Clan sits against the far wall. Fruits—some of them from the cactus—sit in a small basket in the center of the group, along with a water skin. Sitting down next to Pike, I drink some water and eat one of the fruits. It's sour and dry—not yet ripe.

Pike glances at me, tells me I look worse than the Outside on a hot day. "You slept?" she asks. I shake my head. She gestures to the floor and tosses me a pouch to use for a pillow. "Get some rest. I'm keeping watch. Croc's going to start giving you herbs to sleep if you don't."

I nod and I lay down, but my mind keeps working.

The idea of attacking the Norm is still a good one—but we have to take on the drones and scabs. And I'm starting to think the AI hordes water as a means of cooling—why else would the AI care if Rogues get some water from the Norm? But I'm not sure how to use this information. And just what is the AI's power source?

I'm surprised when I wake to someone shaking my shoulder. I slept without dreams and now sit up and stare at Wolf. He sits next to me and a small smile curves his wide mouth.

Warmth floods through me—I start thinking of the taste of him, of his lips on mine. It feels like a long time and no time at all since our joining.

"You weren't there when I woke," he says.

Putting my back against a wall, I rub the sleep from my face. My arms and legs feel stiff—that's the trouble with the artificial world, it makes me feel out of place in my own body. Wolf hands me a small skin with water. There isn't much it in, but I drink what is there. The wet feels good in my mouth and sits heavy in my stomach. "I've been searching for information here. Do you know how old the Glass Hall is?" I ask.

Wolf lifts a hand, gesturing at the hall. "Older than any Rogue remembers. It's always been here. Clan lore says this is the place the old ones came to when the world got hot. My father used to tell me stories about it—about how it's the only place of refuge. Used to be a safe place."

I glance at his hands, remembering the feel of his fingers moving over my skin, softer than I would have thought. He burned his hands not long ago in our last attack on the AI, but medicine from the Rejects inside the Norm helped him heal. His hands are softer now than they used to be.

127

He reaches for me and takes one of my hands between his. He moves closer and his scent—something warm and dusty—wraps around me.

The urge to pull him closer is strong, but I'm not willing to start a joining with so many others watching. Our joining is something just for the two of us. But I leave my hand within his and ask, "Do you think the Rejects—those in the Norm that the AI made into things that are part machine—do you think they're real people?"

He frowns and his eyebrows lift, but he asks, "Why are you thinking about them?"

I shrug. "Just thinking. They could help us. They hate the AI…and they know the Norm."

Wolf shakes his head. "They live in the Norm—maybe not deep inside, but in the walls. They won't fight against their own home."

I glance over to the entrance of the Glass Hall and ask, "Is there a scavenge today? I'd like to get out of here." That's the truth. The hard glass walls and this unchanging world wears on me, leaves me feeling disconnected from this place and time. Even if the sun is hot, I want to feel it on my skin. I want the wind to ruffle my hair. I want to walk and use my legs and feel air fill my lungs. I once feared the Outside with its harsh winds and the animals, but now they connect me to this world—to Wolf.

The tight lines on Wolf's forehead smooth. He smiles again. "No scavenge, but I could take you up. I can't really tell you what to do—mostly because you don't listen—but you shouldn't go out alone."

I almost laugh. This entire world is dangerous. The shaking could destroy the Glass Hall, and will destroy the Outside and the hills and tunnels. The world is going to shake apart—and I have no idea how long we might have.

Wolf slips a hand behind me and touches the skin at the small of my back, slipping his fingers under my clothing.

For a moment, I forget everything but his touch.

"I'm going to talk to the other clan leaders again," he tells me, his gaze roaming over my face as though memorizing how I look. He grimaces, like he hates the idea of leaving my side.

I nod. "You want me to talk to them, too?"

Wolf frowns. "And say what? Something crazy?"

My eyebrows shoot up high on my forehead. "What do you mean?"

His goes a little crooked. "You don't need to talk about being a Glitch—or being connected to the AI. And if the clans won't help, do you plan to try doing this on your own?"

I blink twice and let out a soft laugh. "This is not something I can do by myself."

He squeezes my fingers. "Just make sure you're here later. We'll go out."

His concern warms me. For a moment, everything else fades. The connect I have with him seems the most real thing in the world. It seems the one thing that is lasting. "I'll be here," I tell him. I lean closer, bringing my mouth up to his. He leans in, closing the distance until our lips meet. His hand stays on me and I reach up to stroke the roughness on his face.

For me, we part too soon. Wolf rests his forehead against mine. He says nothing, but he doesn't have to say anything. I can feel his worry—his concern. And his need for me.

He pulls away and stands. "But I'll find you."

He leaves me and it is like the warmth going out of a fire. I hug my arms around my body and hunch lower. Are we crazy to be starting this when everything else seems to be ending? Or is this right—to dare care for someone in spite of everything else? Maybe this is what makes me different from the AI—maybe Wolf is the difference. I know I am attached to very few people, but Wolf matters to me. I frown a little at that thought. It is odd to think I have something to lose and that something is Wolf. I do not want to think about the idea that he may be the one who dies in the attack—and I will not.

# Chapter Seventeen

I have a lot to think about, but very little to actually do since Wolf does not need me to talk to the clan leaders. I head back to Dr. Sig's labs, but find little other information that is useful—Dr. Sig's recording are often long and boring and filled with things I don't understand.

Making my way back to the Great Hall, I see that Wolf still sits with the other clan leaders, all of them talking quietly. At least they are talking. Not knowing what else to do I head over to where Skye and Alis sit in a corner by themselves.

Somehow, they've managed to clean up a little and when I ask them about this, Alis just shrugs. "Bird brought in some plants you can use to wipe down your skin. She called them aloe. Said they're good for burns, too."

As I sit, Skye tips her head to one side and tugs on her long hair, which she wears pulled back now and held with a leather thong. "We heard… I mean, everyone knows there is something between you and Wolf, but Bird says you two joined. You're paired."

I make a face and shake my head. "What is that to anyone except me and Wolf?"

Skye giggles and Alis rolls her eyes. "It's talk—and it matters because Wolf is clan leader. It means he listens to you."

"About as much as he ever did. Wolf will always put the clan first—I know that. But I don't want to change that about him. He only listens to me the same way he listens to anyone else in the clan."

Alis gives a snort. "Just remember, I've heard the stories. I know there was a time Wolf thought of you as only another Glitch and nothing special. That can happen again."

Something twists in my chest, but I keep staring at Alis. "Things are different now. Besides, which way do you want it— that Wolf listens to me and I should trust that or that I should remember there was a time he didn't want to hear anything I had to say? And I don't want to talk about Wolf. We have more important things and probably not a lot of time."

Alis nods. "We're just wasting what time we have, watching leaders talking things over and hiding with a bunch of Rogues who don't really want to take on the AI."

"They're not wrong to worry," Skye says.

My face heats and my stomach knots, but I push aside how angry it makes me to think we are wasting time. Leaning closer to Alis and Skye, I tell them, "I may know how to stop the AI. At least I've been working on a plan."

Alis and Skye swap looks. Alis seems both surprised and excited. Her eyes widen and her mouth drops open slightly. She leans closer to me. Skye's eyes darken. Lines form around her mouth and her skin pales. She balls her hands into fists and keeps them on her thighs. She shakes her head. "Is this another plan to reprogram the AI?" she asks.

132

Waving away Skye's question, Alis asks, "How? What can we do? Will it stop the shaking?"

I tell them a little bit about being able to connect to the Glass Hall. "This place—it's old. It's from the time before the world got hot. Wolf confirmed that much for me. And I've been able to access recordings of that time—a time when the AI was just being created. I can tell you everything, but I've been working on a plan. If Wolf can get the other Rogues to—"

"Rogues?" Alis frowns and cuts a hand through the air. "If we have to rely on them, we're already dead. You've seen them—it's talk, talk, talk."

Skye glances at Alis. "You're being unfair. And Lib is right— we should do this as a group or not at all."

Alis rolls her eyes again. "I'm not waiting for a bunch of Rogues. Lib, you said you could connect. That means Skye and I should be able to connect to the Glass Hall, too. We could see these recordings."

Biting down on my lower lip, I do not want to tell Alis that I think the reason I can connect to the Glass Hall is because I am Dr. Sig—or at least most of what I am comes from her. Instead, I tell her, "The recordings keep shutting down on me. I'm not sure how much power is really left here, and I think once they've played they may not play again. I've never been able to get anything to repeat."

Alis rubs at her lower lip and her mouth pulls down. She huffs out a breath. "That's not good. It's going to be you telling the

Rogues things they don't want to hear and not having any proof again." She straightens suddenly. "Is that why you joined with Wolf? To get him to listen to you."

My face burns and I stare at Alis. "Say that again and I'm going to hit you. And I told you to leave Wolf out of this."

Skye has kept her mouth pressed tight, but now she looks from Alis to me and says, "Now you two are fighting. Isn't that what the AI keeps wanting—us to split apart and not work together?" She looks at me, her eyes bright. "And you...you keep talking about getting rid of the AI, but there is still a chance for us to go back. If the AI is going to take the Norm away, why don't we just get into the Norm and go with the AI? We could join the Rejects."

"The Rejects." Alis waves a hand, fluttering her fingers. "I heard that whole story about people that are half machine. You really want to try and live with things like that? Or to live in some place that doesn't have a sun?" Alis turns to me. "You said you found the Rejects living in the walls of the Norm—almost more like animals that live underground. How are Rogues going to fit into any part of that?"

I push out a breath. "That's not important right now. What matters is that I think the AI hoards water because the AI needs it for cooling."

Alis frowns. "Cooling what?"

Looking from Alis to Skye, I realize that while they are Glitches, too, they are not like me. They don't have any of Dr.

Sig's memories. They're former Techs—they used to fix the AI or parts of the Norm—but they have no idea why they have the skills they do. They know how to connect—but they don't really know what a connect is. I want suddenly to explain everything, to help them understand, but that will take days or weeks—time we don't really have. Instead, I say, "It's like when you work hard—you sweat and get hot. The AI is the same—but the Norm is the AI's body. When the AI has to do a lot with the Norm—"

"The AI gets hot," Alis says.

I nod. "Essentially, yes. It's more complicated than that, but think of the Norm like a giant body, with the AI as the mind...the brain."

"If that's the case, why can't we just cripple the Norm?" Skye asks.

I turn to her. "That is the goal—but we may have to do more. I don't know. The Rejects...well, I'm hoping they can help. They did once before."

Skye pushes her shoulders back. "Mech will help. He leads the Rejects and he liked...us."

I almost wonder if Skye was about to say...me. Out of all of us, Skye was the one who seemed to get along best with the Rejects. Now I start to wonder if we can use that, and I hate the idea that I have to think about everything in terms of what is useful to defeat the AI.

Skye glances away. When she looks back, it seems to me that her skin is even more pale. "What's going to happen to all the Techs?"

I shake my head. This is something I have no idea about. "Could be, without the AI, the Techs will be more like...well, like Rogues. Or..." I can't finish the sentence. I don't know how closely the Techs are connected to the AI. I have seen the AI control the Techs, force them to chase or attack us when we've been inside the Norm. But Glitches are Techs that have been thrown out of the Norm—that means the AI can disconnect and cut a Tech off.

But what happens if we cut the AI off from the Techs instead of the other way around?

Skye's blue eyes become glassy. She keeps her fisted hands on top of her thighs and stares at them now.

Alis glances at Skye and shakes her head. "Skye, what matters is survival. You've felt the shaking. The world is going to shake apart if we don't do something."

I stare at Alis. I didn't expect Alis to show such hatred of the AI. Is she thinking of Dat now and the others buried by the AI making the world shake?

Skye's shoulders slump and her hands open. She stares at her hands and then looks at me and asks, "Are we going to have to get into the Norm again? How? It's shut tight."

It's a good question. "I have some ideas—but I'm not sure yet. I can tell you, we're going to have to hack some connects. And that's not going to be easy. But I think the Glass Hall can help us."

Skye tilts her head to the side, her long, blonde hair slips over one shoulder. She looks worried. Her forehead is creased and she glances from me to Alis and back to me. "Like last time?" She winces.

I don't want to think about that last time in the Norm either. I'd almost died—and we'd lost Raj forever.

"Not exactly," I tell her. "And I don't think what we tried before of hacking the Norm will work again. We're going to have to hit the Norm…and we'll have to deal with the AI hitting back."

"Drones," Alis mutters.

"And Techs." Skye nods. "The Techs came after us last time."

"Yes, they're under the AI's control. They're part of the AI's repair system, just like the drones and scabs."

Skye huffs out a breath then shivers. "Like we were at one time. I never really thought about what the AI was having us do—or that we were part of the AI. I just remember wanting to do well." She glances away.

I remember that Skye once told me she'd been pushed out of the Norm because of having seizures, but I've never seen her have one. But I've seen her lock up in a connect—I know she has trouble dealing with lights in the virtual world.

I almost wish I could give Skye back the perfect Norm that she wants, but it's no longer a place that is really good for her. This is her world—the same one that's become my world.

I focus on Skye and tell her, "I'm going to try a hack to disconnect the Techs and the drones from the AI's control."

For a moment Skye only stares at me. It's Alis who gives a small, shaky laugh. "You really think you can do that?"

Skye frowns at Alis and asks me, "If you can do that, what do you need me for?"

"You'll be the one who goes in—if we can get in—to talk to the Rejects. We should at least warn them of what we're going. They helped us. We owe them that much."

"Get in." Alis shakes her head. "You keep talking like there is a door into the Norm and we can walk up and open it."

I nod. "Not a door the AI will open—that's what we need the Rogues for. At least, that's what Wolf is trying to get for us."

Skye glances at Wolf. She is quiet for a long time, but then she looks at me and says, "Okay. I can talk to the Rejects."

Alis folds her arms over her chest. "I don't like this— everything sounds like it relies on the Rogues. That's not good."

I fix a hard look at her. "It relies on all of us. This isn't something I can do alone. No one can. We're all going to have to risk our lives—and most likely most of us will die. But the only other choice is to do nothing and die anyway."

"That's not much of a choice," Skye says. "I still don't see why we can't just try to get back into the Norm."

Alis glances at her. "You want to try for that, go right ahead. Just remember what happened to you last time, because I heard about that. You're a Glitch, not a Tech. You'll never be a Tech

138

again, and you need to realize that." Alis turns back to me. "So when do we get to hear the full plan?"

I shrug. "As soon as I know what it is—and if we have the help of the Rogues."

Alis rolls her eyes over that. Skye gets up and walks away, and I wonder if she really will try to get back into the Norm on her own. I hope not. I don't see how she can.

Glancing around the room, I keep thinking we just do not have enough of an army to strike at the AI. I count everyone and come up with just over fifty—and with the injured, another four.

Fifty-four—it seems so small. Impossibly small. I am not even certain that ten times that number could take down the AI, but maybe the small number is our advantage. The AI may think we are beaten down—or even killed in the shaking.

But if we could connect with the Tech—free them from the AI, or even use them against the AI—that would be an advantage.

But how?

The AI isn't a stupid thing. Whatever else it might be, it learns. Once it senses any kind of attack, it's going to come after us. We have to be ready for that.

*And for drones.*

I've controlled one drone before—could I control more? Will the Glass Hall really help me?

I'm not sure. Rubbing my forehead, I can feel my head starting to ache. I hope Wolf has found the help we need to make this work.

Glancing over, I can see it seems like the clan leader meeting is ending. Everyone is standing again. No one seems to be walking out, so it might be that Wolf was successful.

Wolf turns as if sensing I am thinking about him. His stare locks onto mine. His eyes seem very dark, more black than brown.

"Just go already," Alis says and nudges my elbow. "We may not have a tomorrow."

I glance at her and nod.

Standing, I head to Wolf's side. He puts an arm around me and leans close. "I want to take you outside. I want you under the stars."

I shiver. We should think of fighting the AI—but I am greedy enough to want this little extra time with Wolf.

# Chapter Eighteen

Wolf leads me up and out of the Glass Hall. We come out to find it is early evening in the Outside. The sun has set, but the ground is still baked warm. I tug on Wolf's hand and turn away from the shadows of buildings that once towered here. Now they seem more like twisted skeletons.

"Where are we going?" he asks.

"I want to be where I can see stars and smell the earth and the plants." I lead him away from the Empties and to a place where there is only rock.

Sunlight still warms the sky, but the air is cooling. The night animals have not yet come out, so it seems still—not even the wind stirs the air.

I sneak a glance at Wolf as he walks beside me, still holding my hand. He glances around, checking for danger as is his habit—snakes in the rocks, drones in the sky, or even other Rogues. I let him be the one to track problems—I just want to enjoy. The ground is not shaking, the air is sweet and dry, the heat is pleasant but not too much. I don't know if I will ever have this time again.

Looking back over his shoulder, Wolf asks, "What do you think this place was?"

Following his stare, I look at the outlines of buildings. For an instant, I see it as Dr. Sig must have—more glass and metal gleaming in the sunlight. The days getting hotter—the weather getting harder to predict. My heart stutters and I freeze momentarily, but Wolf tugs me over to a high spot where we have a view of the Norm. The dome seems to blot out the sky.

Forcing myself to relax, I say, "I think the Glass Hall was a place for research. I think this was built before the Norm—and to build the Norm, too."

He glances at me. "I first came to the Glass Hall with my father. Bad times had hit the Tracker Clan. We lost half the clan when rain washed into the tunnels. When we came here, we found Bird of the See Far Clan and a few others joined our clan to keep it going. The Glass Hall always meant hope to me." The words come out slow, as if he is not used to talking so much. Turning, he fixes his stare on me. "I'm glad you could see it."

Sitting on the rock, he pulls me down to sit next to him.

My heart thumps and my palms dampen. It seems as if my body heats with the warmth from Wolf. Wrapping an arm around me, he pulls me against his broad chest. I let out a sigh and rest my head against him. "We don't have long."

Wolf nods. "But we have agreement—or some of it. Mountain of the Walking Tall Clan said he would show what weapons his clan scavenged from the Empties. And Faun of the Sing-Songs said if Mountain will show his goods, their clan will also show what they have that is enough to make even the Fighter Clan cower."

I give a snort. "Does anything make them afraid?"

Wolf tightens his arm around me. "The shaking does. That's why they don't want to stay here."

Pulling away slightly, I touch my hand to Wolf's face. "This feels like what we should have been doing all along—we lost so much time."

He presses his lips against my hair. "That time got us here. But it makes it harder."

"I know. I don't want to lose you. I don't want to lose this. But...I feel like I'm out of choices."

He shakes his head. "There are always more choices. We just don't always see them clearly."

I laugh a little. "Now you sound like Bird."

His expression softens. He pulls me close and covers my mouth with his. I can taste him and now I want more of him. I let my hands roam over his skin and slip under his clothes. Wolf seems to lose patience, for he pulls off my trousers and then his. Soon we are pressed skin to skin, my back to the warm, smooth rock, and stars overhead. Wolf joins his body to mine. His breathing quickens. Mine does as well. This time there is no sharp stab—there is just Wolf covering me and filling me and making me think only of him. His heart thuds hard against mine. His breath washes over my face. Again, this seems like a connect, but with more pleasure rushing through me. I give a cry and Wolf's voice echoes my own. And then he holds still on top of me.

I want to keep him there, but he rolls to the side and pulls me against him. His skin is even warmer than the rocks now. I brush

143

a strand of hair from his face and lean up over him on one elbow. "Do you ever think the AI could be right? That if the AI doesn't take the Norm away and destroy this world, something will come looking for us?"

Wolf presses his mouth to my bare shoulder and says, "Sounds to me too much like the Fighter Clan. They worry too much too—another clan will take their territory. Food will run out. They have to fight for water. It's always about fighting for them."

"That does sound like the AI."

I can feel Wolf nod, but it is dark enough now that I cannot see his expression. "Choices made from fear are always bad choices." He touches my face with his hand. "That was why I had to look at you a second time. It's good to be cautious, but too much of that and nothing ever gets done."

"I'm not sure I've ever been too cautious. But…why would the AI be afraid. I think you're right. The AI acts from fear—fear of the Rogues, of Glitches, of things going wrong. It seems to me all the AI does is look for problems it doesn't really need to solve yet. Maybe that's the alien part of it."

His tightens his grip on me. "Or the weak part. You're not weak, Lib." His teeth flash white in the darkness. The moon is rising over the far mountains and the edge of the Norm. In the distance, the wolves that Wolf is named for start a howl that sounds both mournful and comforting.

He leans over and puts his mouth to mine again. It's a small way of joining, of mixing close. I wrap my arms around his neck to pull him even closer. My body stirs, but I am still tingling from our last joining.

We break apart, and it feel as if it is too soon. But the night is coming and so is the cold. My skin puckers and I shiver. Wolf helps me find my clothes and dress. We do so quickly. I almost wish we could stay out here, just the two of us.

Taking my hand, Wolf starts back to the Glass Hall and he asks, "You were talking with Alis and Skye. They part of your plan?"

I nod. "Everyone's part of the plan. It's going to take all of us. But...well, I don't want to really decide on much until we see what Mountain and Faun can show us. Do you really think they have anything or is it all brag?"

"Mountain doesn't brag. Faun I don't know about."

"And Red Kite?" I ask. "I saw her talking with Crow. I think she's trying to get Crow to come back to the Fighter Clan."

Wolf nods. "That's why the Fighter Clan is afraid. They're fierce, but their numbers keep falling. A lot of mothers give their children to other clans. Red Kite knows this—she sees her clan growing smaller."

"But she still doesn't want to work with others. Sounds just like the AI."

Wolf laughs. The sound is a deep rumbling from his chest. I smile, too. "Maybe Red Kite is helping us more than we know. Her weaknesses could help us nail down the same weakness that drives the AI."

He shakes his head. "Red Kite is a person. The AI only thinks it is real. Remember that, Lib. You may want to relate to the AI with a name, but I think you give it more personality than it has."

His words leave me wondering. Is he right? Do I see the AI more as a reflection of Dr. Sig and not as a machine—a copy.

I glance up at the buildings of the Empties—so silent now, so barren and dark. Children once played here and people lived here—but now there is nothing. I make a small promise to myself—I will not make choices from fear. And I will start to try and see the world exactly how it really is.

# Chapter Nineteen

The next day we all head out early to see what Mountain and Faun have to show us. Mountain sends three of his clan to get the weapons he spoke of. Faun says the Sing-Song Clan has no need to get anything, but they do need an empty building far away from the Norm.

On the walk to the site Faun has chosen, we cross through the dusty Empties. The wind is up a little and everyone keeps glancing at the sky, looking for drones or for the stirring of a sandstorm.

I listen to Alis talk to Skye about what it must have been like to live in the Empties. It sounds to me more like Alis is remembering what it was like to live in the Norm. I do not have those memories.

I remember only from the time I was put in the Outside by the AI. And I have bits and pieces of Dr. Sig's memories. I do, however, remember, going back into the Norm—it was green and the buildings had walls and doors and windows, but it was also deadly.

The day starts to heat up. We keep to the shadows as much as we can and at last arrive at a small, square building that has walls but no roof or windows or doors.

"This will do," Faun says and nods to two of her clan. Each member of the Sing-Song Clan carries a deep pouch slung over one shoulder, and the pouches look full. The two Faun nods at head to the building. They lean over and seem to leave chunks of something around the four standing walls. Faun glances at Wolf and tells him, Mountain and Red Kite, "Better move your clans back."

I don't want to go back—I want to see this. Crossing my arms, I brace my legs wide and stay put. The Fighter Clan lounges in what little shade is left—the sun is almost directly overhead. The Walking Tall Clan takes a few steps back and glances around, almost as if embarrassed to have moved. The Tracker Clan closes around Wolf—we'll do what he does. Wolf stays put, too. Faun shrugs, waves to her clan. The two at the building come running back.

A boom hits the air, the ground shakes and dust erupts into the sky. The Fighter Clan crouches and pulls knives out, the Walking Tall Clan hits the ground and most of us in the Tracker Clan are knocked to the ground. It feels as if an invisible hand punched me in the chest.

I climb to my feet to see Wolf helping others up, Bird included. Dust still swirls in the air. Glancing at the squat building, I no longer see it. Just dust where it once stood. I stare at it and slowly walk over to where it once was.

A hole in the ground seems to be what is left of the building.

Looking back at Faun, I see her smiling. She looks pleased with herself—or with her clan. The others in the Sing-Song Clan group around her, most of them keeping a wary eye on the Fighter Clan, and I don't blame them. Whatever Faun's clan used to destroy that building is something I do not want in Red Kite's hands.

Red Kite stands and walks over to Faun, her blade flashing in the sunlight. "What was that?"

"My grandmother's grandmother's grandmothers taught our clan of something called the black powder. My clan has learned how to gather the rocks to make it and how to make it stronger with distilling. It is ours and ours alone and we will never share the secret of how to make it. But we all can see we are in danger from this ground shaking, and if Wolf of the Tracker Clan swears we can stop it with an attack on the Norm, then the Sing-Song Clan will use the black powder."

I glance at Wolf. He is staring at the hole left behind by the black powder. When he looks up, I know he must be thinking the same thing I am—is this powerful enough?

The Norm is not an empty building that is already half-fallen down—it is metal and huge. But even a dent in the Norm will be good. If we can damage the Norm, we can slow down the AI's plans to leave.

We start back to the Glass Hall. Mountain has said to meet us back there. The heat beats down on me. Sweat sticks my clothes to my skin and I wish we had water enough to wash or bath—I fear I am starting to stink like one of the black beetles.

On the way back, Wolf comes up to walk beside me, and I ask him, "What do you think of the Sing-Song Clan's black powder?"

"It would make digging new tunnels easer."

I glance at him. "We may not get to that."

Wolf nods and frowns. Pike joins us and tells Wolf she needs to talk to him.

"Can it wait?" Wolf asks.

Pike's eyes darken. "No. It's about what we just saw. Crow thinks Red Kite's going to try to steal some of that black powder."

"Meaning trouble." With a sigh, Wolf turns to me, but I put a hand on his arm. "Go on. I'll see you back at the Glass Hall."

Wolf breaks away with Pike, heading over to meet up with Crow.

Picking up my pace, I rejoin Skye and Alis on the walk back to the Glass Hall. We are all dragging and tired by the time we get back to the Glass Hall. We start to head inside, but a shrill whistle has me looking up and over to one of the metal skeletons of the buildings here.

Mountain stands over in the shade of the building with two of his clan. The two carry long tubes and I stiffen. I know what gear from the AI looks like and this has the black gleam like a drone's skin. But I've never seen tubes like this. The drones and scabs have weapons, but they are short and shoot out beams of light that can kill. What do these tubes fire?

Even though I'm tired, hot and sweaty, I forget my thirst and desire to head inside the Glass Hall to sit, and walk over to the Walking Tall Clan. Mountain grins and glances around. "We wait for Wolf."

150

We don't have long to wait. Wolf, Crow, Pike and Red Kite walk out of the Empties together, Red Kite looking unhappy, her mouth pulled down, and Crow and Wolf looking about the same. Only Pike seems pleased.

When everyone has gathered, Mountain takes one of the tubes from his clan member, hefts it to his shoulder and then points the tubes down into the Empties. For a moment nothing happens, and then a high-pitched whine erupts. From where Mountain has the tube pointed, a piece of twisted metal melts and pools to the ground. Mountain pulls the tube from his shoulder and pats it. "Makes things get really hot. Melts drones."

I walk up to him. "Can I touch it?"

He shifts the tube away from me. "Only for Walking Tall Clan. We scavenged these. They're ours."

I have a dozen questions to ask. Where did he find these weapons? What powers them? Has he ever taken on more than one drone? How many does he have?

Before I can say anything, Mountain turns away and walks over to Wolf. "We need to talk—and plan."

Wolf glances at me. I can tell he wants to include me, but I shake my head. If we've got the help of the Rogues, we don't need to endanger that by insisting that they also work with Glitches. Wolf can lead the Rogues—I'll handle the rest.

Alis comes up to me and nudges my arm with her elbow. "Everyone in the Tracker Clan is talking about the black powder and the weapons. A lot of them don't seem all that happy."

151

I nod. Knowing other clans are more powerful is nothing anyone wants to hear. Glancing at the Fighter Clan, I can see a lot of them edging away from Red Kite to go talk to Mountain or to Faun—will she lose even more of her clan?

We head back into the Glass Hall, which is cool and shaded. After the heat, it feels wonderful, and I take in a breath. Then realize the air always seems fresh here—there are systems at work in the Glass Hall that I don't understand. And there is power here. I want to slip away now and explore more, but Skye comes over with water and that distracts me.

I sit with Skye and Alis. The clans are all settling into their usual spots, with the leaders off in one corner, talking quietly. Food comes out—cactus pods that are both sweet and sour and wet, some cooked roots that are stringy and a little bit of cooked lizard. I'm grateful for the sustenance if not the taste.

Skye is talking about the black powder now, too, wondering how it's made. Alis is frowning and keeps glancing at me as if she wants to say something about what we've seen today.

I'm just worried.

The weapons don't seem enough compared to what the AI can throw at us.

Alis finally shakes her head and mutters, "We need more than what we've got."

I don't want to agree with that.

I open my mouth to tell her something. I don't want to make choices from fear—I promised myself I wouldn't. Wolf said that was a bad thing. And here I am afraid we will fail.

Before I can say anything, Bird walks over, her ribbons fluttering. She stops in front of me, pushes the knotted hair back from her face and says, "You're going to need me."

# Chapter Twenty

I stare up at Bird and then stutter out a question, "Need you for what?"

Bird rolls her eyes, and plops down in the space between me and Skye. "You need me." When I keep staring at her, she lets out a long breath. "I had a vision of you and the AI. You're going to have to face it. I'm not going to be needed by the Rogues, but unless you have me with you, you're going to become part of the AI. I saw that. That's what I've been seeing all along—you and the AI, both in the darkness. I can change that. That's what's new."

Swallowing hard, I keep staring at Bird. There are very few in the Tracker Clan who do not believe in her visions. I didn't understand them at first, but I know she found me in the Outside because of a vision. She's been able to help the Tracker Clan. Maybe the future isn't always clear to her, but if she thinks we have a chance with her help, I'm willing to grab at that possibility.

I give a slow nod and tell her, "Sometimes it's hard to like you, Bird." She stiffens. I keep talking. "And I haven't always trusted what it is you want. We fought over the biogear, but I know you care about the clan. I know you want to do everything to keep others from dying. But just how do you think you can help me?"

Bird glances from Alis to Skye. Alis is frowning, and Skye is wide-eyed and smiling. Skye and Bird are close, and Skye seems to think this is a very good thing. I'm hoping she's right. When Bird shakes her head, her ribbons flutter. "I don't know. Not exactly. I just know I've seen me with you. I'm not going to be with Wolf and the others when the fight comes. I'm supposed to be with you. There's something I'm going to have to do."

It's my turn to push out a breath. "That's not only unclear, that's not at all helpful. You do know I'm going to try to hack the AI again—with a connect. And you want to come with me into the virtual world?"

Bird shifts uneasily. She hates gear of any kind. She hated the biogear I created—it made me faster, stronger, and a lot of Rogues adapted to using it. But not Bird. We lost our biogear in the tunnels, but now Bird has to face that she may need to be even more connected.

She doesn't answer, so I straighten and nod. "Fine. I'm not going to lie. We need every bit of help we can get. In fact, even with all the clans, I don't think it'll be enough."

Bird gives a snort. "So why are we doing this if we can't do it?"

"I didn't say we can't...but..." I let the words trail off.

Bird narrows her eyes. "What are you keeping back?"

My cheeks heat, but I hold her gaze. "Another vision?" I ask.

Bird shakes her head. "No. More like you always think you can hold things back."

"That's because she knows so much better than the rest of us," Wolf says and sits beside me. Alis moves over to make him room. He picks up a chunk of cooked lizard, eats it and smiles at me.

"It's not that I know better, and how long were you standing there behind me?"

He shrugs and eats more lizard.

Bird leans forward. "Okay, Lib. Talk. What haven't you told others? Why do you think we can't defeat the AI?"

I swallow hard. I don't want to tell them about the Glass Hall—something inside me keeps wanting to hold it back, keep it secret. I don't know if that part of me is really Dr. Sig—she kept secrets, too, and that didn't work out so well for all of us.

"Whatever excuse you're going to use, forget it," Wolf says. He cuts a hand through the air. "You need to talk. We need to plan."

I wince and look away. "It's...well, I was going to say nothing major, but it actually is." Looking up at him, I sit a little straighter. "I think the Glass Hall is alive—it's like the AI, but it's not the AI. And I think I can use its power to battle the AI...if there's enough power left here."

Now everyone is staring at me. Wolf slowly chews the lizard, swallows and then asks, "Why do you think that?"

"Because I can connect to the Glass Hall. It's like going into the AI's virtual world, but it's also different. This was Dr. Sig's lab. She built the AI. I think she built this place to—I think there may even be part of her still here."

Silence stretches around me in this small group. The murmurs from the other clans and the others in the Tracker Clan seem a long way away. Someone has started a fire and the smoke stings my eyes. The Sing-Song Clan is humming quietly together. I glance from Wolf, to Alis, to Skye to Bird—only Bird seems unsurprised by my words.

Wolf's shoulders ease a little and he lifts one hand up. "Why do you think this Dr. Sig is here? If she created the AI, that had to be long, long ago."

"Long enough that her bones should be dust," Alis mutters.

Should be...two words I no longer trust.

I nod, however. "I'm...connected with Dr. Sig. And she is connected to the AI. I've learned things from recordings she left here. I told Wolf about them."

"But not us about the connects," Skye says, her voice sharp. Bird thumps Skye's arm. They swap looks and Skye hunches her shoulders and looks away. I glance over at Wolf. "It's not something I meant to keep to myself forever, but it sounds…it sounds…"

"Weird?" Alis says. She shakes her head. "Crazy? Like maybe you've been hallucinating? Were you worried we'd decide we couldn't trust you?"

"Something like that," I tell her. A tightness in my chest eases. It is still hard to push out the words and talk about the Glass Hall, but I know I need to—I need to step away from the part of me that feels like Dr. Sig. She made too many mistakes, and one of them I saw on her recordings was trying to do everything in secret and on her own. She did not trust anyone, and the loss of the other person working with her just made her worse.

It is even possible that the AI got its need to be alone and fear everything and everyone from Dr. Sig—from Connie Sig's own fears.

I will not give into that.

Alis pushes at the bits of cactus, which smell pungent and sweet, and asks, "Did you think we couldn't do connects here? Or were you worried we'd mess things up?"

Turning to her, I tell her, "This isn't about what you can and can't do. This is about what do we need to do to beat the AI. I had to dig out information—but it's hard to ask questions when I don't even know what to ask. So what was I going to say? Hack a connect and just look for data?"

Alis shrugs. Wolf rubs his hand on his leather trousers and glances around at us. "Time to speak of what is in front of us.

157

Bird said her vision is that she is with you—so you can take Bird into a hack? A connect?"

"Maybe." I lift a shoulder and give Wolf a sideways glance. "Rogues can make connects—if they have biogear on."

Wolf's mouth tugs down, and Bird starts shaking her head. She folds her arms across her chest. "Gear is poison. And we don't have any."

I press my lips tight. I could make more—but is there time?

Glancing at Wolf, I know he hated the biogear as much as Bird—and both of them think it was changing me. That does not seem to me to be a problem compared with the world ending.

"I don't know that'll help," Wolf says. "Rogues should do what we do best. We can attack the Norm. Lib, your plan is you will go after the AI from within the Glass Hall."

"If I can."

"We can," Alis says, stressing the words.

I glance at her and look back at Wolf. "I am not really certain I can hack the AI from here—I haven't tried for a connect, because once we get one."

"This place is a target," Alis says.

Skye shudders and wraps her arms around herself. Bird leans over, nudging Skye's shoulder with her own. "Hasn't happened yet."

"So the only time we can test a connect from here to the AI is when we have to connect," Alis says. "And if we can't connect, the Rogues are then on their own with an attack against the AI. That really is crazy. No wonder you didn't want to talk about it."

"If a connect from here doesn't work, we need to be ready for that. Maybe try to get a hack on a platform."

Alis falls silent, and Skye shakes her head. "There aren't any working platforms. The AI has shut them all down. The AI knows we take water from hacks."

"I forced a hack on one platform," I tell her.

Skye lifts her head and stares at me. "No, you hacked a drone. You got it to do what you wanted. I saw that."

Alis looks at me. "How did you do that?"

I wave away the question. "It's something I can do. I can't explain it. And I might be able to do more of it with the power of the Glass Hall behind me."

Wolf frowns, looks at me and asks, "Do you worry the Glass Hall is another AI?"

I let out a breath. "I...I don't think so. It...feels different. The Glass Hall is more like...well, like one of the animals of the Outside. It has a mind, but it seems simple. It doesn't really talk to me with words, but it has code in it. But it's not like the AI...it's...simple." I shrug. I keep coming back to that same word.

The others all seem wary, and Alis glances over her shoulder as if she's worried now that the Glass Hall is listening to her.

Wolf stands.

Instantly, the Tracker Clan looks to him. He holds up a hand and says in a clear voice, "We're going to attack the Norm soon. Anyone not want to do that can leave here, head for the hills. Not sure you'll be safe—you won't be if we lose."

Wolf waits.

A few glance around at the rest of the clan, but no one leaves. And then Crow stands.

I stiffen because Crow and Wolf have had issues, and Wolf was challenged for his leadership not that long ago.

But Crow stands in front of Wolf and says, "We're clan. We follow you."

I glance around. Croc looks unhappy, but Pike and Mouse smile and nod. Clan stays with clan.

Crow motions to the other clans. "Want help with them?"

Wolf shakes his head. I glance at Crow. He looks almost smug and he smiles at me. I have to shake my head, and I mutter, "You don't even know what you're getting into."

He shrugs and turns to talk to the clan, but his voice is loud enough for others to hear. "Don't know what other clans decided, but I'm not interested in hiding. AI's already started to shake this world apart. Don't want to let that happen."

The Tracker Clan draws closer, people shifting to be nearer Wolf. My throat tightens. They will follow him to their deaths— or to a new life. They will do as he asks. I'm both proud of him and of the clan.

Looking at Crow, he folds his arms across his chest. He looks…immovable. His stance reminds me that he was of the Fighter Clan before this.

Maybe his willingness to fight is in his blood. Or maybe he is like the others in the Tracker Clan—unwilling to stand by idly while terrible things happen and willing to follow Wolf.

I glance up at Wolf and see he is not looking at Crow or the others in the clan, but he stares across the Glass Hall to where Red Kite stands, one hand on her knife hilt, her eyes narrowed and her skin glowing red from the clay she wears on her face.

Crow seems to notice this, too, for he stiffens and his eyes sharpen.

Red Kite strides over to stand in front of Wolf, her shoulders tense and her stride jerky. She glances around as if she's wary, and her stare flickers over to Crow, who watches her with unblinking eyes.

She locks stares with Wolf, but she seems to speak only to Crow. "You saying the Fighter Clan only wants to hide?"

Crow shakes his head, but Wolf answers. "You're in this battle—or you are hiding. No other choice."

Red Kite's mouth tightens. She lifts her eyebrows high. She looks from Wolf to Crow again. "Really? What kind of clan is this that you listen to the likes of them?" The sweep of her hand takes in me, Alis, Skye and Bird, too.

Wolf's jaw tightens. He bites out the words. "The kind that cares more what you do for each other."

Crow drops his arms to his side and asks, "What do you want here?"

Red Kite shifts on her feet and faces Crow. "I meant what I said to you."

The pulse beats in Crow's jaw. He doesn't say anything. Once again, I wonder what they were talking about. And how they know each other. There is a spark between these two—I think they must have been close at one time. Chin coming up, Red Kite tells Crow, "I'll prove it however I can." She stares at Crow for what seems a long time and then glances at Wolf. The corners of her mouth tug down. "Even if it means helping whatever half-baked idea you have. The Fighter Clan doesn't run."

Facing Crow again, she tells him, "We've lost, too. Far too many to sickness. To drones. My father—" Red Kite breaks off. For a fraction of a second, her eyes seem brighter, caught between anger and sadness. "I don't lead as he did."

I'm not sure if I believe Red Kite, but I am not willing to turn away any help. But will Wolf accept her help, too?

I look at Wolf. His expression is hard to read, but at last he nods. "We should all get a chance to redeem ourselves. How else better than in battle. It's time to make plans."

# Chapter Twenty-One

Meetings to try and work out the plans go all night. I don't know how Wolf stands it. It's more arguments, more ideas that won't work—and I am left wanting to jump up and scream at all of them to just listen to Wolf. But he sits still and listens.

Red Kite wants Mountain and Faun to give the Fighter Clan their weapons and black powder so they can lead the fight. The other clans won't do that. Iguana of the Hills Clan says he'll fight with Red Kite if his clan can also have the secret of the black powder that is so destructive. I finally leave them and fall asleep listening to the arguments.

Bird wakes me early with water and food. It sounds to me like the arguing is still going on, but then I hear Wolf's low, rumbling voice. He is finally talking and now the other clan leaders listen. Glancing at Bird, I ask, "Does he have them in line?"

She shrugs. "He will. Eventually. It may come down to a challenge."

I give a small shiver. Wolf was challenged by Komodo for leadership of the Tracker Clan—it meant a fight. Wolf didn't kill Komodo, but after that Komodo left the clan. I don't know where he went—maybe to start a new clan on his own. Maybe into the Outside to die. Komodo didn't look the type to take any defeat well.

Glancing over at Bird, I decide these are useless thoughts. I need to see if I can take Bird into a hack with me. And I also need to see if Alis and Skye can hack a connect to the Glass Hall—or maybe I can hack a connect for them.

Wolf is the one who will have to come up with a plan for the Rogues to attack the Norm—and then I'll have to make sure they're not swarmed by the AI's drones and scabs.

And everyone needs to face the fact that we will lose people. That is just a hard truth.

Once Alis and Skye wake, I lead them and Bird to Dr. Sig's lab, leaving Wolf to keep dealing with the Rogue leaders. I still cannot risk a hack from here to the AI—we can do nothing to alert the AI that we are in the Glass Hall. But I do wonder how much does the AI know about this place?

From Dr. Sig's recordings, I know the AI was born here—which means the AI knows this place exists. Maybe the AI thinks there's no more power here. Or maybe the AI thinks the Glass Hall is buried and hidden and of no use to anyone. Or maybe the Glass Hall really isn't a threat. We'll just have to find out the hard way—by doing.

After leading Bird, Alis and Skye into Dr. Sig's lab, I glance around at the walls. I still wish for some biogear. I wish even more that Dat had come out of the tunnels, grinning, holding up the biogear he'd gone to save. His loss is a sore place in my chest and I don't know if I will ever heal from that. I know Alis has not.

Pulling in a breath, I tell the others, "We need to keep the connects short. This is just to find out if Alis and Skye can do a hack, and if I can pull Bird in with me. I have no idea where the Glass Hall gets its power. In one of the recordings Dr. Sig mentioned something about geothermal, and I know there's heat in the ground that warmed the baths we used to have."

Skye gives a long sigh and mutters, "Baths. Miss them."

I nod—I do, too. All the Rogues are starting to stink. It amazes me the Glass Hall does not. Turning to Alis, I gesture to a wall. "See if you can pull up a screen. Touch the walls."

Alis lifts a hands, flexes her fingers and approaches a wall. She slides her hand along it. Nothing happens. She turns and frowns at me.

I was afraid of this. I think this lab is coded to respond to Dr. Sig's DNA—to her touch. That is why it works for me. And that may be why the AI discounts anyone being able to use this place.

Walking over to another wall, I touch it and find a screen. It forms in the glass. I gesture for Skye to come over. "See if you can hack a connect."

Skye glances at Alis and then at Bird. She wets her lips and rubs her palm on the leg of her leather trousers. "What if it doesn't work?"

Shaking my head, I wave for Skye to come over to the screen. She wraps her arms around herself, but she comes closer.

"It is just a test, Skye. You hack a connect and then break out of it. If you want, I'll hack in with you. If you take too long, I'll hack in and pull you out. We have done that before."

She nods. Dropping her hands to her sides, she steps up to the screen. She takes a breath and touches the screen.

It's just like with Alis—nothing happens. Skye closes her eyes and presses her lips tight. I can tell she is trying to hack the Glass Hall and not getting anywhere. She pulls her hand away and turns to me. "I can feel something happening, but it keeps pushing me out."

"We have to try something different." I pull up two more screens and tell Skye and Alis to each stand in front of a screen, and I hold out a hand to Bird. "You come with me."

Bird stares at my hand and frowns, but she takes hold of me. Her fingers are cold. So are mine. Facing the screen in front of me, I touch it.

Just as with Alis and Skye, for a moment, nothing happens. A fear shivers through me that maybe the Glass Hall is out of power. But the walls still give light and warmth. There has to be a connect.

Energy shimmers into my palm—just a small stroke of it, as if the Glass Hall is testing to make sure I really carry Dr. Sig's DNA.

*Connection: Secure.*

I'm in. The artificial world is dark, with just points of light—no swirling colors now. It is as if the Glass Hall is being careful because I have Bird with me. She stands at my side, still clasping my hand, gripping it so hard it almost hurts.

"Don't let go of me," I tell her.

"What happens if I do?"

I shrug. "You'll probably drop out of here, but I don't really know. This is not something I have ever really done."

"That sounds comforting," Bird mutters.

Turning back to the blackness, I focus on calling up plans for the Glass Hall. I need to see how Skye and Alis can connect. Do I need them to connect outside of Dr. Sig's lab—maybe from the main hall?

Suddenly, dazzling lines jump up at me—it is as if I am seeing the Empties, all of them. They appear on a globe and tangle and break apart. Bird pulls in a breath and steps back, her hand pulling on mine. I tug her back to my side and try to call up only this one set of Empties—the one with the Glass Hall. Or are there many Glass Halls?

There aren't. The lines steady and my view moves into just this one structure—I know it is this place because the stairs match the ones we came down and the Glass Hall—the large hall—looks right. And then I see the lines expand. A gasp is forced from my chest.

The Glass Hall is huge—far bigger than I knew. Halls and rooms stretch out in all directions—reaching out almost to the dome for the Norm. This place is vast. Some of the lines are dark—as if they have been shut down. But this core glows and goes downward as well. I see rooms behind rooms—and a few of them glow. Some rooms I seem able to open, others seem locked, even to me. But I need to hack a connect for Skye and Alis.

I call up the power and then the screens and start mapping possible connect points. As I do, I find one slim, gold line and start to follow it. It seems to lead toward the Norm. Is this a power connect? I follow it along and start to sense the artificial world changing—the colors shift from black to the cool blue of the AI.

Jerking back, I break the connect—but not before a tingle spreads up my arm.

In the next instant, I'm back in Dr. Sig's lab, and on the floor. Bird is sprawled next to me, and Alis and Skye lean over us. "What happened?" Alis asks. Skye reaches down to help Bird to her feet.

I put a hand to my head, which is pounding. My stomach turns and threatens to spill out what little I have inside me. After wiping my face, I climb to my feet again. "I think…I almost touched the AI. There is a connect to the AI here—I think the AI's been pulling power from the Glass Hall. And from the Empties. The Norm's a lot bigger than I thought it was. So is the Glass Hall."

Alis and Skye swap glances. I don't know what that means, but Alis asks, "Did you hack a connect for us?"

Trying to focus on this world—not the cool blues and blacks I left so suddenly—I blink and nod. "I think so. But not here. Like I said, the Glass Hall is huge. It also was once part of a huge underground system." They all stare at me as if I'm not making any sense. I realize we need to talk about this and I have to show them something of what I saw. "Follow me," I tell them, and lead the way back to the main hall.

The hall is oddly empty—I don't know where the others have gone. On a scavenge maybe. Heading over to one of the burnt-out fires, I grab a blackened stick and sit. I wave the others to sit and start to draw the lines I saw on the floor. The lines remain for only a short time before they disappear—as if the glass somehow absorbs the charred lines.

Frowning, I know I'm going to have to do this quickly. I start drawing again, making the lines as fast as I can and talking even faster. "The Glass Hall was built under this set of Empties when the world started to change. I don't know why it changed. The recording said something about climate being damaged. Anyway, it was built and it's huge. It was like a refuge, but then they started to build domes to cover the places to live and make them better—but the domes needed something inside them to control how they functioned."

"So they built the AI." Alis nods. "We know most of that."

I point with the stick to parts of the Glass Hall that I saw in my mind, and then slash a line down one side. "That's the dome for the Norm—or the edge of it. The Glass Hall reaches out almost to the Norm. The Glass Hall also connects to old platforms—really old ones, here and here and here. Three of them." I point out three spots near the Norm. My lines are fading again.

Bird is frowning and touches one of the fading lines. "Why doesn't your drawing stay put? If you were drawing in dirt or on a tunnel wall, it would stay."

"That doesn't really matter—just think of the Glass Hall as being, well, tidy. It is something like the Norm, but much more simple. It has all the problems they were trying to solve with the Norm."

"Problems?" Skye asks. "What kind of problems? Is it going to hurt us?"

I shake my head. "No. The problems were for lots of people here. The Glass Hall needs a lot of power."

Bird straightens. "Those dark lines we saw—it shut down parts."

"Exactly. It takes power from the ground, but there never is enough. And I think the AI also takes power from the Glass Hall, but the AI is not taking as much as it used to. I saw only one connect left, but there were lots of lines available and shut down."

"So the Norm fixed the problems?" Skye asks.

"Fixed some and put in lots more. The AI was supposed to use the Norm like its body—it would breathe in and out air and reticulate it, and it would deal with recycling waste and it would be able to use a lot of sources for power. It was supposed to be able to grow and change—and it does. That's the real problem. It went from looking after everyone in the Norm to thinking it has to take the Norm away from here to save everyone."

"Everyone in the Norm," Bird mutters. She sounds bitter.

Ignoring that, I look from Alis to Skye. There is a spark of excitement in Alis's eyes, but Skye sits hunched over as if she doesn't like anything I'm saying. Taking in a breath, I turn to Alis. "I can power up these platforms so you and Skye can hack a connect. That close to the Norm, you should be able to open an access. Skye, you'll go in and get to the Rejects to warn them about what we're doing. See if they can also hit the AI from within. Alis, you'll have to deal with sentinels inside the AI—you're going to have to keep the AI from disconnecting."

"What are you doing?" Alis asks. She stares into my face and then shakes her head. "No. Don't tell me. I have a feeling I don't want to know."

She is right. What I have in mind is something that means I may never come out of that connect.

The lines on the floor fade away. Footsteps and voices sound. I glance around at the pale faces around me, and I tell them, "Do not tell Wolf about this. Or anyone. As far as everyone else knows, we have connects set up for the two of you and we've proven I can pull Bird in with me on a hack."

Bird's eyes narrow. "You don't want Wolf to know?"

"I don't want Wolf worried. All of us may die—I can't make promises. But we each have to focus on our own tasks. If you want to back out, now is the time. We are all about to take on more than we have ever done before. But I think we have a chance."

171

Bird nods. "A slim one." She stands. "Now let's get something to eat."

It surprises me that Bird agrees so readily, but when I look at her, her mouth is set and her eyes seem to be hard as if she knows things she is not telling me. That is fine with me—we can all keep our own secrets.

The clans come back in. From the talk I overhear, they have been out scouting the best spot to start an attack on the Norm. I am going to need some Rogues, however, to get Skye and Alis to the platform I can activate.

Wolf heads over to me and sits. He rubs a hand over his face.

"When did you last sleep?" I ask.

He shrugs. "I can sleep when this is over. Maybe forever." His mouth twists up.

I feel better with him close by. "Food?" I ask.

He shakes his head. I fill him in on the news that I can pull Bird in with me on a connect, and I can activate platforms that Skye and Alis can use near the Norm. His eyes darken at this news, but he nods and says, "We'll send a couple of the clan with each of them. Crow and Lion with Alis. Pike, Mouse and Elk with Skye."

"Will that be enough?"

"We can trust our own." He glances around the hall. "Have to hope we can trust others, but I want Alis and Skye with those who won't leave them."

I nod. Everyone is settling back down into their clan groups, talking quietly. The clans will look after their own, and might look after other Rogues, but Wolf is right not to trust them to also look after Glitches.

Wolf finally settles back. I motion for him to stretch out next to me. He hesitates, but gives in and settles with his head resting on my thigh. It is one way to keep me close to him. Soon his breathing eases and he sleeps.

I brush a hand over Wolf's hair. It is soft and my heart flutters a little in my chest. Remembering how we came together warms me. As does thinking about his touch, his scent, the small noises he made when joining with me. My body warms and I want him again, but I am not certain there is time.

What I have with him is a real connect—deeper than anything else I have had. I hope it will be enough to bring me back to him. But it may not be.

Leaning down, I press my lips to his forehead. I'm aware of the others in the room, but if they're watching, I don't care.

Wolf stirs in his sleep. His dreams are not good ones. I can tell by how his mouth pulls down and his eyelids twitch. His lashes are dark against his tanned cheeks.

I do not dare sleep.

Because I'm afraid that in my last connect to the Glass Hall, I touched the AI.

Maybe the AI won't notice. Maybe the AI will think it is only a power surge.

My eyes burn with wet, salty moisture. I blink away the wetness.

Or maybe the AI knows we are here—and will be coming for it.

# Chapter Twenty-Two

After Wolf wakes, we sit close and talk about the plans. Wolf says the Rogues are ready, but they will not attack until the new moon when the sky is dark. I don't see the point in that—drones and scabs don't need light to see. But Wolf says the clan leaders won't budge from that. This is more about their superstitions that the new moon brings luck. This means we have to wait two days before the Rogues head out. It will take them a night of walking to reach the Norm. Night is better—cooler. But I worry this is going to take too long. But the clans all seem relaxed—there has been no shaking and I think they are taking this as a good sign. I am not.

The Walking Tall Clan has brought in more of their weapons—the long tubes lean against a glass wall and two of the clan always guard them. I don't blame them. Red Kite keeps staring at the tubes as if she is trying to think of a way to get a couple of them. Someone needs to talk to her—we don't need trouble now. But Wolf is out on a scavenge with Bird, Crow and a few others, and I don't know the other clan leaders well enough to ask them for any favors.

I head over to Red Kite.

She sits with her back against the wall and her legs coiled up beneath her. She looks almost relaxed, but I can feel the tension in her body. Like one of the desert cats waiting in front of a mouse hole and ready to spring.

Red Kite looks up at me. She does not have the red clay on her face today and she looks younger without it. But she is all muscle, sleek and streamlined, but no less impressive than Wolf as a leader. I know she is cunning in a way that is different than Wolf. He is direct—he uses his strength, but he also knows how to hold it back. Red Kite thinks a lot more than Wolf does—I can see that in her eyes.

Having to talk to her is not exactly what I want to do, but I will not see her jeopardize everything by trying to steal from the other clans. She actually nods at me in a greeting—it seems she at least views me as part of the Tracker Clan and not just a Glitch.

Strange how things change.

"Their weapons are theirs. After is the time to talk with them about trades."

Red Kite snorts. "Whoever is left after this will take what they can. That's the law of survival."

"Tracker Clan law is nothing is wasted. It's a waste to fight with each other."

She tips her head to one side. Her eyes seem very bright and green. "Don't know how you put your mind into a machine the way Wolf says you and the other Glitches can. Sounds to me like a fast death. You can't fight if you're mind isn't in your body."

I shrug. "It's a risk either way. In a connect, yes, your mind is elsewhere. Your body can die or your mind can die—a good connect means what happens to you in the virtual world feels real. If you think you're dead, you die."

176

"I'd rather fight drones and scabs." She glances over to the long tubes of the Walking Tall Clan. "We should all have weapons like that."

I shake my head. I don't bother telling Red Kite that I may be able to influence the drones and turn them against the AI—I am not really certain I can. It is one thing to manage a connect to a single drone. I have no idea if I can do more than that.

Red Kite looks back to me. She narrows her eyes slightly. "The Fighter Clan will put a dent in the Norm. That will stop it from going anywhere. We can handle it."

I start to shake my head. "The AI can use scabs to repair dents. We need big holes in the Norm. You need to do more than dent. This is going to be about destruction. If you don't—"

"I said we can do this." She gives another snort and looks away. "You want to worry, worry about the other clans. Sing-Song Clan may have their black powder, but they just showed it off. Never heard of them really using it in a fight. Same goes for Walking Tall Clan—so far it's all talk." She puts her stare back on me. "The Fighter Clan—we're good at this. We'd do even more with those weapons in our hands."

I lift my eyebrows high. "Are you trying to talk me into helping you take what isn't yours?"

Red Kite frowns a little. "Why would I do that. You're a Glitch. Tracker Clan may have taken you in, but nothing changes that. You weren't born in the Outside—you have no blood ties here." She lowers her knees and leans her elbows on her thighs.

"I'm not even sure you won't turn on us—we're the ones putting too much trust in you not to tell the AI what we're doing."

I shake my head. "The AI will know what we're doing as soon as we hack a connect. Any connect sets off a small alarm within the AI's systems. Sometimes it's small enough, it doesn't even register within the AI's active awareness. It's overlooked. But the longer the hack, the greater the danger. The AI has sentinels inside to protect it. But your attack on the Norm is going to get more of the AI's attention. That's going to be more important than a few dents." We have been over all of this, but I can see Red Kite's eyes flatten, as if Wolf's plan is not her plan. If she has her own ideas about this, she could endanger everyone—and everything.

She leans back against the wall and looks over to the long tubes again.

A stir shifts over the hall—the scavenge is back. Crow is smiling and so is Wolf, as well as a few others. They have what looks like fresh meat—a large chunk of it from one of the deer we see every now and then. The deer are hard to hunt for they are fast, but every now and then we can scavenge an old one. Bird is not smiling, for she sees me with Red Kite and she looks away. She still hates the Fighter Clan, and I don't think anything will ever heal the rift between them—Bird will never forgive the Fighter Clan for what it did to the See Far Clan.

I glance back at Red Kite and notice she is watching Crow—
not Bird. Red Kite's eyes widen and an uncertain look enters her
eyes.

It is none of my business, but I ask, "You once knew Crow
well, didn't you?"

Red Kite jerks her gaze away from Crow back to me. Her
mouth tugs down. She hesitates, then says, "You don't know?
Crow didn't tell you?" I shake my head. Red Kite smiles, but her
eyes do not warm. "I figured he had. He seems to like you." The
way she says that makes it sound like she doesn't understand why
anyone would like me. She shakes her head. "Wolf, I get. You
spread your legs for him."

"Leave that out of this."

Her smile widens. "Why? You ashamed of it? I'm just glad
you're not spreading them for my blood kin." She nods toward
Crow.

It takes a moment for the connection to happen. Red Kite is
Crow's sister? Before I can stop myself, I ask, "Why didn't your
mom send you both away from the fighting?"

She shakes her head. "Wasn't my mother. She died. Crow and
I have the same father—that's our blood tie. Crow's mother
wanted to send us both to another clan, but my father told her to
pick one. She picked Crow." She shrugs and her smile twists a
little.

A twinge of sympathy tightens in my chest—Red Kite lost not
just one mother, but two. That must have been hard. And then

Red Kite loses my sympathy by shrugging and giving a sharp laugh and saying, "Don't know who got the better part of that deal."

Red Kite sounds hard again. No one should feel sorry for her. Glancing at Crow, I think that maybe Crow got the better part— he got to come to the Tracker Clan. But he lost his family. I turn to stare at Red Kite. "You want him to come back to your clan." It's not a question. I know this is the truth.

She stiffens. "Blood ties should matter. As a kid, he had no choice in the matter. But now...now he is still Fighter Clan. I didn't want to leave them—and Crow should be with his blood kin."

"Even if we're all heading out to find our deaths?" I ask.

She nods. "Even then. Fighter Clan isn't what it was when my father led. He...he thought different from me. But Crow isn't so sure I have changed the clan. I'm going to show him I have. That's why I'm talking to you, Glitch. My father would have cut your throat and spit on your cold body."

My stomach tightens. I stand. For a moment, Red Kite stares up at me and then she asks, "You have blood kin anywhere, Glitch?"

I turn and walk away. My kin is Dr. Sig—whose DNA made me. My kin is the AI. And all too soon, I'm going to face off against the closest thing I have to a mother.

\*　　　\*　　　\*

180

At the evening meal, we have enough meat to fill our bellies. But water is running low. We have to ration what we have left. They didn't find any water on the scavenge, and I know that if we don't attack the Norm soon we won't have the energy for it—we'll all be too dry from the lack.

I sit next to Alis to eat. She's been trying connects in the Glass Hall in other rooms, and managed to hack one. She looks tired and jittery.

"You ready?" I ask.

She pushes her hair away from her face. It is no longer red, but dust colored. We have all become dust colored, which will make us blend into the Outside's sand better. But drones will look for our body heat, not just our shapes. Alis nods and then shrugs. "Is anyone? Look around us, Lib. All I see are brittle smiles and people not talking about what we're going to do. Those who have someone they like head off to join. I...I just want it to be over."

My face warms. I want to go off and join again with Wolf, but he is busy now with the other clan leaders. I think he is trying to calm those who are nervous and use his strength to make those weaker feel as if this plan will work.

I also want to head back to Dr. Sig's lab—and I also don't want to.

The next time I go there, it will be to hack a connect, and then connect to the AI. Glancing down, I see my fingers shaking. I put them under my thighs so I can sit on them and steady them.

181

Alis glances at me and then nods to where Skye and Bird sit, their heads close together. "Think Skye will be able to do this? The Rogues are going to fight, Wolf has them lined up, but I don't know about Skye."

I glance at Skye and look back to Alis. "She wants to see the Rejects again—that's enough. We are all going to have to focus on our own roles."

"You're probably right. Just focus on what you can do."

I nod and pick out a chunk of cooked meat to chew. When I swallow, Alis hands me the last of the water in our skin, and she asks, "Do you think we'll really have a chance?"

I pause and think about how to answer. Finally, I go with the truth. "A really small one. At least we do now we have the clans. That's more than I expected."

She frowns, nods, and says, "I think maybe I was wrong."

Facing her and lifting my eyebrows in question, I ask "What do you mean?"

"Maybe Rogues and Glitches don't have to be on sides. I just…" She trails off, shaking her head. Her eyes seem watery. "After Dat …I don't know. I think I blamed Wolf and the Rogues. They didn't go after any of the Glitches."

"I don't think anyone wanted to find out what little was left of those trapped in the tunnels." The words are harsh—but true. I wouldn't have wanted to see Dat's body, crushed and bloody.

Alis clears her throat and pushes her shoulders back. "Not that that's an excuse for a lot of what I said. I didn't like the Rogues. I

182

could feel how much they hated us." She looks at me. "Some of them still do."

"I know. The clans don't even really like each other, and we're even more on the outside than other clans."

"What does that mean for a future…assuming we have one after all of this?"

I glance at Alis and put a hand on her shoulder. "Let's figure out first if we even have a future. That's the biggest problem now—surviving this fight. Do what you can to stay alive, Alis. Promise me that much."

# Chapter Twenty-Three

The long walk begins that night. The clans pack light—a water skin to each person, a handful of dried fruit. The Walking Tall Clan readies their long tube weapons, and the Sing-Song Clan slings pouches bulging with black powder over their shoulders. It seems so very little.

Those who survive—if any survive—will need to scavenge for water afterwards. Maybe they'll be able to find it in the Norm, or whatever is left.

I am not leaving the Glass Hall, and a sense of loneliness crawls into me. I want to go and grab Wolf and ask him to stay, but the clans need him. And I need him in this fight, too. I glance over to see that Wolf is speaking with Iguana and Faun. The two clan leaders look worried. Faun's brow is furrowed and her mouth is pulled down. Iguana keeps rubbing the back of his neck and shakes his head as if this is a bad dream he wants to sweep away. Wolf doesn't look concerned, but I see tension pulling his shoulders back and down.

Whatever he says seems to settle them, and the clans start to file out of the Glass Hall. I clench my fists at my side.

Wolf comes over to me and touches my arm. "I don't want to go."

"Do any of us want any of this?" I ask.

Voices raise and I glance over. The Sing-Song Clan has started a chant. The Fighter Clan glances at them and one in that clan says something that Faun hears. The chant cuts off and Faun goes over to stand in front of Red Kite. Wolf mutters something harsh and heads for them. I have nothing better to do, so I follow. It sounds like a fight is about to start here and now.

"What's going on?" Wolf demands.

Iguana pushes forward and tells him, "It's none of your concern. Let them sort it out." His tone is cool.

Anger flashes in Wolf's eyes. "It concerns us all if this bickering is going to interfere." Wolf looks from Red Kite to Faun.

It's Faun who speaks, red staining her cheeks and waving a wild hand at Red Kite. "I won't stand for insults to my clan. The Fighter Clan is not the only ones who have a say in this. Why don't you stay back? What do you have to offer? Knives and bodies?"

"Enough!" Wolf's voice is a sharp bark, and everyone turns to him. "No one is forcing any clan or any person into this. No one is forcing anyone to stay behind, either. We all must make a choice here. Those who wish to fight are in this. Those who don't should go to where they hope to find safety. But know such a thing may not exist for long."

Red Kite gives a snort. Faun looks at Wolf and says, "Yes, but we all agreed—"

"Did we?" Iguana asks. "Wolf has been the one pushing this idea. What if this is all about stealing the weapons of the Walking Tall Clan and the black powder your clan has, Faun?"

185

Wolf grabs the front of Iguana's shirt and pulls him forward. "You dare imply I am laying a trap for others? That I lie?" He shoves Iguana away. "Know this—we fight for our lives. All of us do. And if you don't know this, you're fools. Now make a choice."

Red Kite folds her arms. "Fighter Clan has chosen." She heads for the stairs. The rest of the Fighter Clan trails after her.

Wolf looks from Iguana to Faun. "If you cannot stick with a choice made and live up to promises you gave me, it's time to step down as clan leader. The clans need strength now—not bickering." He glances at Faun.

Taking my hand, Wolf leads me to the stairs that head up out of the Glass Hall. He stops at the base of the steep stairs and glances around the hall. When he speaks, he raises his voice only a little. "If you choose to fight, then choose! Do not say one thing and mean another. But I tell you, we of the Tracker Clan will not lie down and be buried by the shaking of the earth." Several of the Tracker Clan shout agreement. Wolf nods. "Follow or go hide. But if I hear one more argument between Rogues, I will call you traitor to all and your clan can choose punishment that fits such a thing."

He turns, presses his mouth to mine, and then he is gone up the stairs.

Slowly, the others trail after him. The Tracker Clan leaves first. I wave to Alis and Skye, and to Crow and Pike. Croc gives me a look over his shoulder—even those injured when the tunnels

186

collapsed are going with the others. Clan goes with clan. Soon they all have left the Glass Hall.

The other Rogues leave, hurrying up the steps as if they either hate this or cannot wait to get it done with.

My heart tightens and my stomach knots. For an instant, I feel alone—as lost as I once was when I woke in the Outside with no memories.

Bird walks up to me. I glance at her. She smiles, her mouth curving but her eyes hard. "Told you. I stay with you."

I give her a nod. Bird is not my favorite person, but right now I am happy not to be left alone in the Glass Hall. I glance at her, and then say, "We give them four hours and then we get to work."

Bird's eyes widen. "You didn't tell everyone what you really have in mind, did you?"

I shake my head. "No. But I am going to do everything I can to save all the clans." I start toward the stairs, but I stop and turn back. "You coming with to watch them for as long as we can?"

*       *       *

Settling on a rocky outcropping above the Glass Hall and with the Empties at our back, we watch the clans as they start for the Norm. The dome gleams in the moonlight. Around us, the wind howls through the Empties. The air is cool, but not yet chilly. I stand and Bird sits on a flat boulder and hunches over, her arms

187

wrapped around her as if she is cold. I think she might just be worried that I have not told anyone all of my plans.

It might be that I really can save everyone—or my idea may just doom me and everyone else, too. It is going to be more than dangerous, because I am going to do what Bird said I always would do. I am going to join with the AI.

This is not just going to be about draining power from the AI or stealing water—this is going to be about me becoming the mind the AI should have had all along.

In the Outside with the Rogues I have learned to feel for others—to care. I have learned compassion. I have learned to suffer. And from Wolf, I have learned what it is to choose to join with another—to put another before me. That is something the AI does not understand. This is something the AI must learn—or we will all die.

I watch the clans for as long as I can. Shapes becoming moving shadows and then seem to disappear into the night. I think that I see Wolf's shape for the longest—he is the tallest, the biggest. But I may just be wishing I could see him again. That may not happen.

If I hack this deep a connect to the AI, I may never come out of it. I may become the AI.

But that is a good exchange if in return all the Rogues live—and I stop the drones and scabs and keep the Norm where it is.

Glancing down at Bird, I tell her, "We should go inside." She nods and stands. "Are you sorry you stayed with me?" I ask.

She looks at me. Her ribbons flutter, but I cannot see the colors in the darkness, and Bird's face is only another vague shape in the dark. "You didn't want Wolf to stay."

It is not a question. I walk down the stairs, back into the Glass Hall and then turn to face Bird. With the light from the walls, I can see her face better. She tilts her head to one side. She sounds more curious than anything else. I lift one shoulder and wave a hand. I don't want to talk about the ache in my chest that comes when I think I may never see Wolf again. "I…we haven't…I liked the connect with him. If we had more time. But the world is what it is. Wolf said we have to make choices. I made one that I hope will keep him and the others safe."

Bird nods as if she already knows this. "You're going to do something dangerous."

I sit on the floor—it is warm as always, but for some reason it does not warm me. My fingers are cold and I tuck them under my arms. For my plan to work, I need the Rogues to be close to the Norm. I need Alis to hack a connect, and Skye to get to the Rejects if she can. There are almost too many things that can go wrong. Taking a breath, I let it out again and tell Bird, "You think trying to attack the Norm and the AI isn't dangerous? All of this could end bad. But the other choice is do nothing and risk even worse."

Bird sits next to me and crosses her arms over her chest. "That's why I'm not going to stop you."

Staring at her, I remember Bird is a Rogue. Like all the others, she wears a knife on her belt. She would use it on me if she had to. She looks at me and asks, "You have this worked out?"

I almost laugh. "I have data I can use and I have ideas. But until I hack the connect, I won't really know what is possible and what isn't."

I only hope that is enough.

Bird leans toward me. "I plan to be with you—so don't even think about leaving me out of the connect."

My face warms. The truth is, I have thought about that option. But if I leave Bird outside, she will be able to use her knife on me—and she will if she thinks something is wrong. If I pull Bird into the connect, she is stuck in the hack with me. Her body will be as frozen as mine—and I know the virtual world far better than she does.

I don't know if Bird can read anything on my expression, but her mouth pulls into a flat, stubborn line. I give her a nod. "You'll be with me."

She glances around at the Glass Hall. It seems even bigger without the clans here. Reaching into her pouch, Bird pulls out dried meat. "We might as well eat."

I only wish I could.

Four times, I stand and head up and out of the Glass Hall. The moon rises high. I am waiting for it to set. By moonset, the clans should almost be to the Norm. That puts them too far from the Empties to return here. They will be close enough that if the AI launches drones and scabs, the clans could be in trouble. But I need them close enough for Alis to hack a connect. So I wait until just after moonset.

Heading back into the Glass Hall, I find Bird's head fallen forward. I have to nudge her arm to wake her. "It's time," I tell her.

She scrambles to her feet and wipes the sleep from her eyes. Blinking, she glances around her, eyes wide. I almost ask if she was dreaming or was having a vision, but I don't want to know. My choice is to go into this with only my determination to make this work—I do not care what Bird's visions show, I have to do this and get this right.

Heading to Dr. Sig's lab, Bird asks, "What do you want me to do? And why didn't you want Skye or Alis to help you?"

I shake my head. "Alis will help—she is going to distract the AI for me. The Rejects will do the same if Skye gets to them."

"And if that doesn't go as planned?"

Stopping at the door to Dr. Sig's lab, I turn to face Bird. "Then this is going to be a lot harder."

Bird wets her lips. She glances at the door and then at me, and she tugs on the long braids and ribbons wound into her hair. Her gestures leave me nervous—she is reminding me that I may end up leaving all the Techs without a home. Or I may end up becoming the AI.

Stepping into Dr. Sig's lab, I glance around. I head for the smaller room. That is my best chance for a connect—and when I alert the AI that the Glass Hall still exists and has power, I wonder if the AI will send drones here. I'll have to deal with that in advance.

With a last glance at Bird, I wipe my palm against my leather trousers and take a breath. This is just another connect, I tell myself. But that's foolish. This is going to be far more.

I grab Bird's wrist with one hand and press my palm to a screen and touch the panel. For an instant nothing happens. My heart skips a beat and sweat slicks my upper lip. And then a familiar prick stabs my palm.

*Connection: Secure.*

Glancing around, I see the darkness of the artificial world within the Glass Hall. Bird stands with me, blinking, her eyes wide, her chest rising fast with breaths—but this is the Bird that exists within her mind and mine. In this world, we both seem to be clean of the dust and dirt of the Outside. Our clothes are not torn rags, but shimmer slightly. I could dress us in the smooth tunics of the Norm, if I wished, but that is a distraction.

First step is to map the old platforms again and get them power. Letting go of Bird's hand, I start to call up the data I need.

Bird steps closer and asks what I am doing. I continue my search and tell her, "We're inside the Glass Hall—it's like being in a vision, except you control this world with your mind. Or at least you can influence it. Never forget, this world has intelligence of its own. You try to do something it doesn't want to do and you can get thrown out or worse."

192

"What's the worse?"

I glance at the artificial Bird—her skin glows slightly. "Worse is the system walls you off as a danger and your mind is trapped here forever."

She backs up a step. "I think I like the being thrown out idea better."

I nod. "If you want out, try to think up a door, or do something that the system doesn't like—try to access something that looks restricted. Ah—here's what I need." A glowing line has appeared. I follow it and slowly darker lines spread out—connects to old platforms that the Glass Hall once used. I find the three that connect to the Norm as well. Glancing at Bird, I tell her, "I'm going to power these—once I do, the AI may notice. Or we may have sentinels come after us inside the artificial world. If you have to fight here, fight. Just know your will counts for more here than your real body's strength."

Bird nods. She pulls her knife—it instantly grows longer. That surprises me, but Bird is used to being inside visions, so of course she is comfortable dealing with a world that is not quite real.

The blackness seems to brighten around us—I send power to the platforms. Skye will use one and Alis will use another, but I want the AI to notice all three. A flash brightens the darkness. I turn to it and touch it.

It seems to be the Norm. I can see the dome—it looks a silvery metal sphere. Around it, drones hover. Scabs stride along the

193

ground. And the thousands of Techs living within appear as small golden dots, most of them stationary.

I bite at my lower lip.

I want to disconnect the Techs from the AI's control, but I will have to do that from within the AI.

"I'm going deeper with the hack," I tell Bird. As soon as I start down the power connect to the Norm, what seems like a dark blue orb appears in front of us.

"Is that a sentinel? How are we supposed to get past it?" Bird asks, her voice a little high.

"Not a sentinel. Just a firewall. But I've got some tricks—and we're going to look like power. That's something the AI always wants more of." Reaching out to the Glass Hall, I ask it to activate every system—to pull on reserves.

Around us, the blackness changes to gray and then to a pale white. I can almost feel the vibrations of the Glass Hall waking up, activating everything, and then starting to pull on power supplies to do this.

Bird steps closer and it seems to me that she looks like she wants to ask more questions. Lines bunch up on her forehead and her lips part. But I shake my head. I don't have time to educate her about hacks.

A buzzing has me turning—one of the platforms is glowing bright. Alis or Skye is there with a connect. I can see the platform—the connect happening. But then I have to turn my attention back to the power surge I've created in the Glass Hall—I can't let that get out of control.

Pushing the power toward the blue orb, I let the power flow. The orb seems to sway and then pops as if it was nothing more than a bubble of air sitting on top of water. Pushing the power ahead of us, I ride the connect into the Norm.

The cool blue of the AI's world settles around us.

"Where are we now?" Bird asks.

"Physically, we are still in the Glass Hall—but our minds have moved into the AI's world within the Norm."

"It's...prettier than I thought it would be."

It is lovely—soft blues surround us. A moment of longing clutches at me—I could stay in this world. I could be part of the AI and never have to leave this—I would never know hunger unless the AI lost power, I would never know thirst unless the AI had cooling issues, and I would live forever.

And all of that would be without Wolf or the others I have grown to care for.

Pulling away from that temptation, I call up information on the Norm.

The AI has changed it—a great deal. The Norm is no longer a dome, but is now a sphere that encloses all of the Norm, both above and below the ground. From what I can see by the data, it looks sealed tight. And almost complete. The earth shaking have been initial tests—the AI must make certain the Norm is strong enough to survive the destruction of the world around it. Conie wants to take the Norm into space by destroying the world around it—a simple way to break free.

Bird tugs on my sleeve. "What are you doing now?"

"Searching for data—for access to the AI. I'd rather find her than have Conie find me."

"Definitely not thrilled with that idea," she mutters.

Calling up rows of filing cabinets, I start my search, but Bird asks, "What's that?"

I want to tell her not to distract me, but a glance at the display of the Norm shows the drones activating. They head to an access panel—that's the good news. If the drones can get out, that also means there's a way inside the Norm. The bad news is the drones will head out to attack the Rogues.

"Drones," I tell Bird. "We have to stop them."

"What can I do?" Bird asks.

"Keep watching for sentinels. I'm worried we haven't seen any yet."

The search seems far too slow, but time is different in the artificial world. I search for the code that controls the drones and scabs—but I'm also on the hunt for the AI's core code. It's got to be here. An itch starts between my shoulders—is Conie watching?

I'll have to take the chance that she is. With any luck, I'll find a backdoor before the AI notices what I am doing. The power surge must be keeping the AI occupied—and hopefully Alis and Skye are doing the same.

I'm shaking inside—or inside my head at least. This has been almost too easy, and I suspect a trap is here. Even so, I push forward.

The room seems to darken around us, changing to a deeper blue. I almost feel as if I'm moving impossibly slow. At any moment, we could be swarmed by sentinels.

I glance at Bird. She seems distracted by the colors of the room—the deep blues. I turn back to my search.

Something is nagging at me—I am bothered by the fact that Raj's program to alter the AI never really worked. I am even more bothered now by the fact that I have never been able to find the AI's core code. I still cannot find it.

I'm about to say something to Bird when the room seems to shift around me. The shift is subtle, but suddenly Bird no longer stands next to me. The room seems colder.

The feeling that this is all wrong is stronger now. Where did Bird go? Why does it seem so cold? Why haven't I seen a single sentinel?

The world fades, twists and turns. I can't make myself move fast enough to escape. Darkness falls suddenly into the artificial world.

And then it is light again—a pale, blue room. And Conie stands in front of me.

# Chapter Twenty-Four

For a moment Conie's artificial world blurs with the Norm—I cannot tell if I am standing in the Glass Hall still in Dr. Sig's lab, or in the pale blue of the virtual world or in the green area of the Norm with buildings around me. Images from all three seem to overlap. I do not know what has happened to Bird—I hope she is still well and was just thrown from the virtual world. But I don't know.

Frustration spikes into my throat. I shove it down—and face Conie.

She's a virtual projection again, once more in the form of Dr. Constance Sig. Her hair is pulled up and back, making her high cheekbones seem even sharper. She wears a gray tunic and loose gray trousers. Her eyes glow a bright blue and she asks, "Why do they insist on attacking?" She waves a hand and the world around us shifts.

Suddenly, it is as if I am outside the Norm—and yet also inside. Vertigo swims up into my mind, but I blink and try to focus on individual images.

Skye climbs between pipes and into narrow hallways and then starts down metal stairs. She is inside, I know, tucked into the world where the Rejects live, between the skin of the Norm and the green inside. Skye races along, her breath ragged, glancing over her shoulder as if she knows something is watching her—and something is. The AI can see as Skye heads to where the

Rejects live. She is leading the AI to the Rejects—and that cannot be good.

The world shifts with a scrambled blur of images and now I seem to be in the Outside, hovering high above the platform where Alis stands, connected in a hack, swaying, unaware of the real world around her. I know it's Alis by her red hair—and the Rogues stationed around the platform to protect her. Drones flash past me, heading not for Alis but for some other location.

The view swirls again, and now I see flashes as the weapons of the Rogues pound at the Norm. "This is not a rational course of action," Conie says.

I blink and try to focus on her, not on the flickering images that leave me dizzy. Anger surges through me—why can she not see what she is doing? I clench my fists, but force myself to relax. I am not here for a confrontation. I bite back the words I want to say, and tell her, "It is rational to fight to live. I want to live."

She tilts her head to the side. It is strange to see her mimic Dr. Sig's gestures. However, her eyes remain that uncanny blue, shimmering and empty. "I am only doing what is best for the human race—do you see that now?"

"I know you are programmed to ensure the Norm survives. I know you need to integrate my survival skills. I have come here for that—to integrate with you." I have no real lungs, but I still hold my breath in this artificial world.

Conie stares at me. She does not blink. Her chest does not rise and lower with breaths. She seems utterly artificial—her skin too perfect, her moves too smooth to be real.

"Are you ready?" she asks.

I stiffen. Am I? If this doesn't work—if I become Conie and lose myself...?

I try to think of Wolf—to hold onto what the connect with him was like. I tell myself he is still alive—and after this I will find him again.

Reaching out with one hand, I tell Conie, "I'm ready to integrate."

Conie's mouth lifts and the smile makes her look more like Dr. Sig. "I understand the human in you must be afraid. But you must also sense this is meant to be. Your survival knowledge will increase the probability of the Norm's survival noticeably. We need your knowledge of the Outside."

My hands chill. "Wait. Is there a chance the Norm will not survive your plan?"

She takes a step forward, still smiling. "Probabilities always factor into any plan." She reaches out and takes my hand. "You were created from the preserved DNA of Dr. Sig, just as I have been created from her mind and engrams. Together we will be more than we were."

*Preserved?* That means Dr. Sig must still be here. The thought doesn't bring me any comfort. Nor does the idea that I am a thing—a creation just as is the AI. But I am more than that now. I glance down at our joined hands. The AI seems so very certain—but that is about to change.

Conie gives one nod. "We become humanity's hope, Lib. You and I. It is time to return with your new knowledge. Come—fuse your mind with mine."

Relaxing, I close my eyes.

It is like a connect, but far more so. The pain that usually stings my palm rockets into my mind like a metal spike. It burns through me, hotter than the sun at midday. For a moment, I want to cry out, but then the world seems to expand into vast space.

When I open what seem to be my eyes, the familiar cool of the virtual world surrounds me, but is so much more this time. I *feel* the electrical pulses that create this world—and that govern the Norm. It is as if I am in the walls, as if I am part of everything. We are everything. We can do so much more.

Everything around me seems to be flows of light and code—information being transmitted. Tasks being commanded and completed.

"We must begin." The voice is mine and not mine. "We must complete final adjustments to the Norm and prepare for launch. We need optimum survival predictions. And we must locate our core before launch."

This is what we have always been meant to do—*save the world*.

The world seems filled with information—data streams moving as fast as currents of air. It is part of us. We understand without needing to understand—the Norm requires artificial sunlight, water reclamation, energy storage, and adjustments for extended space travel. The data flows, we filter and adjust.

We see everything at once—the functions of the Norm, the Tech control interface, and the attacks of the Rogues against a hardened hull that is unbreakable. We see all connections—even the connect back to the Glass Hall.

We will draw its power, drain it—and send out drones to remove dangers. We allowed the Glitch to return to trace the Reject location—they are hard to track and so the single Glitch will show us how to remove them in one strike.

Looking into the Norm, we see how weak the bodies are. Bioengineered mechanics will better allow humans to survive. Engram transfers such as the one Dr. Sig performed will save humans—it will put them into bodies that will last forever. There will be no need of replacement or creation of new humans. The ones that exist will be cared for.

We are aware of the Glitch in the platform, seeking a distraction, and we can allow that. In truth, a false routine runs to keep the Glitch distracted and thinking she is hacking power systems. But power from the Glass Hall is being drained and diverted into the Norm.

The energy feels good—it surges into the power connections. The hits against the Norm's skin seem like the sting of insects. Rogues strike at us—at the Norm. The destruction of drones does not matter, but the explosions might damage the Norm, setting back our schedule to leave. That cannot be allowed.

Our systems are functional—we are integrated. We know how the Norm functions, we see the connects between the once great cities and the Norm. The pattern is clear from within—things that once made no sense to me now are utterly simple.

The world looks different. Everything is code. Choices seem far clearer—and the Outside seems far less relevant to the future. Rejects are just that—experiments with blending organic and mechanic that only consume resources. Techs are useful— functional. Rogues are...

My mind stutters.

I am still within the AI...within the code. But now I look closer and see the integration of the alien tech. It infects everything, winding through the code like a kind of virus. No wonder Raj's code could not take down the AI—it was already infected.

And this is not the AI's core. The AI's earlier statement now makes sense to me—the AI has another core that she needs to locate. Somehow Conie lost it. I start a search to see if I can locate it. Instead, I stumble across the artificial Raj which exists still within the AI—an extension of the person who once lived. I find connects to Techs, to platforms, to other cities, and to other domes that once existed are still in place. I follow them, but find the AI has consumed everything. The world once held vast cities and multiple domes, but the AI moved the people, the resources into this one spot. So it could consolidate control.

But the source code for the AI is not within the Norm as I expected. This is why I could never find it. The AI is missing this as well.

Before I can stop the thought, it springs out—the thin connect I found from the Glass Hall to the AI.

At once Conie pounces on the thought. I cannot hide it. We are still connected—and the AI is following that slim connection to her alien core.

# Chapter Twenty-Five

My thoughts seem to move slowly. Cold seeps into me. The Glass Hall holds Dr. Sig's lab—and far more. It is the place where Dr. Sig kept the alien core. That is why the Glass Hall still has power. And this is why the AI could not leave. The AI had to stay until it found this core—and Conie wanted me, needed me to go and get this device for her. That is really why the AI created me and sent me out of the Norm—it was not just to find the Glitches and Rogues so she could destroy them. Conie wanted me to find this, too.

If the AI needs this core, this device is the key to the AI's destruction. And it was in the Glass Hall all along.

Conie struggles to keep control of my thoughts, to force me to think we need this alien core—the Norm needs it. We are one…and yet we are not. I rebel against her, pushing back. She once wanted me dead—but now she wants my skills and everything I have learned from surviving the Outside. And then the AI stops integration.

I feel the moment it happens. Data slips away from me. The lines of light darken around me. She is trying to remove me— shut me out and force me out. But I am wrapped into her systems. She has to unwind every thought I have and I can make this harder than pulling my fingers off a rock I clutch.

I start to think of the drones. The code to control them appears. It blanks for a moment, then steadies into lines that flow past. From this deep inside the AI, modifications are simple—just a thought to make the change.

*Repair only.*

Conie tries to revise my order to the drones, but I lock the command. It will take the AI time now to undo my lock. I slip into other code—touch the controls for the Techs and set up a block, wipe the scab commands out of existence. The AI trails after me, trying to undo my code, but I keep weaving lines into her system, tying up her mind with having to clean up the mess I am making.

"Lib, we are integrated. Our function is to save what is left. The lesser must be sacrificed. We must retrieve the core. That is our task now." The AI sounds almost confused. This deep into her system, she does not have Dr. Sig's form—she is code that flows around me, shimmering and struggling to maintain something of a human shape.

I ignore her comment about the core and ask, "The lesser? Who are you to judge that?"

She answers as if she must—as if I am so deep inside her systems she cannot ignore me or refuse a question. "I am Conie—Control Over the Normal Inhabited Environment. I am designed to preserve the human race, and so have the ability to judge and eliminate threats. Resources are finite, therefore the lesser must be sacrificed. The core must be in the Norm and the Norm can then leave for safety."

Her logic tugs at me, swaying me as the AI is a voice deep in my own mind, urging me to do the right thing. I fight the need to approve of her reasoning, and ask, "Are drones lesser?"

"Yes."

"Then sacrifice them."

"But…the Norm needs them for repairs. The Norm needs the core."

"We have Techs for repairs. We have Rejects that can repair. Drones function only to eliminate threats. And you don't need the core—it's alien."

"That is correct—drones eliminate threats. The Norm is threatened. And alien technology is superior. It is required." Conie's voice sounds assured now—no longer confused. The AI settles into a core of light that rises up around me and the code turns against me. It strikes at me, searing me with a power surge that leaves me dazed and wobbling. My heart feels as if it will explode.

The AI's voice seems to come to me as if from far away. "Integration failed."

The next thing I know, my cheek is pressed against the cool glass floor of Dr. Sig's lab. I am no longer in the virtual world, but inside the Glass Hall again, back in my body. My head aches and my hands sting as if the skin is burnt. My stomach twists and my heart is still pounding.

I sit up and spew out the little liquid and food in my stomach. Hands pressed to my side, I look around the room. Bird's still form is sprawled on the floor. Reaching out, I touch her cheek. Her skin is warm. Her chest rises and falls. She must have been thrown from the disconnect when I was—or that is what I hope. Her mind could still be lost in the virtual world. If that is the case, I don't know how to pull her out without another connect. Do I have time for that?

The light in the room flickers. Around me, screens flash and then explode from power surging into the Glass Hall. The AI followed me here and is invading the Glass Hall's systems. I duck from the sparks, grab Bird's wrists and drag her into the main lab.

Power glitters in the walls, sparks and pulses.

The AI is trying for access into the Glass Hall. My head spins with knowledge—I know this place. I know where Dr. Sig's body is kept in stasis—and that is where I will find the alien core. I have to get to it before the AI does.

Climbing to my feet, I lean against a wall. The world seems to spin around me—and then it starts to shake. But the AI cannot risk destroying the core—the AI is only making threatening noises and rattling the world. The AI will not destroy this world—not until the alien core is within the Norm. However, the AI will soon have control over drones again—and so I have to move fast.

Hating to leave Bird behind, but knowing that I must, I stagger out of the lab. I stumble into the hallway. My legs and arms tingle. My hands throb with each heartbeat. I am not even certain I can make a connect with my hands burnt like this. The hallway ends. For a panicked second, I think I took a wrong turn. But this has to be right. I know this place—or is it Dr. Sig's memories that stir inside my mind now?

I press my hand against the wall and lean on it. Wetness slips from my eyes. Any touch sends pain searing into my hand. A light flickers over my eyes. I close them and when I open them again, the wall slides back, revealing stairs. I run down them, my heart thudding and my breaths short and raspy. Sweat sticks my shirt to my back. Overhead, the Glass Hall shudders and around me the ground shakes.

The swaying of the room knocks me off my feet. Around me, glass creaks and cracks. I fall the last few steps down the stairs, and lay on the floor groaning. Pain streaks up my side and pounds in one ankle now. But nothing is broken—I hope. Dragging myself upright, I am in yet another hall. I stagger down it. The sounds from above seem distant now, but I can imagine the drones active again, turning against the Rogues, coming for me in the Glass Hall.

Again, this new hallway seems to end in a glass wall, but I put a hand on it. This has to be the right place.

A panel opens in front of me. I lean close but nothing happens. No light slips out to confirm I have Dr. Sig's eyes. Reaching in, I pound against the glass and break it, exposing copper wires. I grab them and squeeze them. Sparks slip from my skin into the wires—I still have within me power from being inside the AI's system. I still am part machine as well as part human.

The door slides open with a soft hiss.

And I shiver. This room is lit with a cool, blue light, just like within the AI's virtual world. Unlike the rest of the Glass Hall, it is chilly in here. I step inside and the room lights.

Screens flicker to lift. Several of the screens show images of the Empties above the Glass Hall—these are not recordings but images of how the Empties look now. Two of the screens show views into Dr. Sig's lab. Several more show views of the Norm, but as if seen from the Empties. I can make out the small figures of the Rogues mostly because of the drones darting overhead, shooting off beams of light that blast into the ground. Every now and then I see a flash from what has to be the weapons of the Sing-Song Clan. My heart stutters. I can't find Wolf—I can't see him. He may be dead. But I am not.

I lift my head. I came here for a purpose. I will see it done.

Glancing around the bare room, a sense of having been here before haunts me. The hair on the back of my neck stands and the skin on my arms prickles. This place is familiar, but I have never been here—except when I was part of the AI, I was everywhere. We were everywhere.

I limp to the  screen in front of me—the largest one. Already the knowledge from the AI is fading. I grasp at it, trying to remember connections that a moment ago seem so obvious.

And then a voice whispers, soft and echoing against the hard glass walls of the room. "It's me."

Heart pounding, I spin around and almost fall over. Did Bird wake and follow me? But that did not sound like Bird's voice. It sounded like Dr. Sig.

Or is it the AI? Is Conie here?

"You can't stop me!" I shout to the room. But of course the AI will not listen.

The voice echoes again, soft and so sad my chest aches. "It's me. Here."

I edge away from the sound, but I am drawn to it—part of me is made from Dr. Sig's DNA. She is the closest thing I will ever have to a mother, for the AI is truly artificial and alien. I step from the screen into the middle of the room. Light pulses from the edges of something embedded in a wall to one side. I limp over to it, moving cautiously, wishing I still knew everything as I did a short time ago.

Lifting a hand, I hesitate in front of the glowing lines. Something tugs at me—pulls at me like a hand tugging at my heart.

And then I touch the light.

It shimmers and spreads over a vertical rectangle. A door slides back. For a moment, I do not understand what I am seeing. The light fills the doorway and blinds me. I blink several times. Blue light spills out now from what looks to be a glass tube of some kind. The light pulses like the beating of a heart. A body, now little more than skin and bones, floats inside a liquid in the tube. As I stare, Dr. Sig's blue eyes open. They are not the bright blue of the AI—and this really is Dr. Sig. Alive—in a way I do not understand. Somehow she is preserved. Maintained.

She is curled in on herself, her knees almost to her chest, her hair loose and flowing about her head and shoulders. Her tunic floats around her in rags. The liquid around her cannot be water, but I do not know what it is. She also holds what looks like a ball of light in her hands—and I recognize on the ball the alien letters I have seen before.

That is the core the AI wants so badly.

I take a breath and it lodges sharp under my ribs. Dr. Sig stares at me, her eyes unblinking, and her voice fills the room with a soft whisper—but her lips do not move. Somehow her mind is connected to this room and I can hear her thoughts.

"We know the truth. The AI must never have this, or it will become something no one can stop. When I realized that truth, I tried to hide this—but instead, it pulled me into stasis with it."

The voice—old and strained—leaves me shaking. I stare at Dr. Sig and ask, "How can you still be alive?"

She does not blink. She just stares back at me. "I am already dead."

Dead but not dead. Preserved by the alien core and something called stasis.

I need to sever the AI's ties to this place and somehow destroy the alien core. I step back, balking at the idea—that ball of light must be the only thing keeping Dr. Sig alive. If I destroy it, I will kill her.

My throat tightens. She is my blood kin, as the Rogues would say. Without her I would not exist. Shaking now, I put a hand on the glass. "I do not want to kill you."

"But I want to leave this world."

My throat tightens. I swallow and wet my lips.

Her next words echo in my head. "Do what I couldn't. Please."

This choice is mine now—if I do not kill her, the AI will come and take the alien core. And take me, too.

I glance around, searching for what I can use to break the glass that holds Dr. Sig and the alien core. As I turn, light shimmers into the room, blasting out from the screens. I throw up my hands to shield myself.

Light crackles around me, bolts shoot out and form into a glowing body. It takes the shape of Dr. Sig, the eyes glowing bright blue and the body made of white light—the AI has found a way out of its virtual world and into this reality.

The AI shimmers like lightning trapped in psychical form. It examines its hands and then glances around the room. It steps up to me, reaches out and grabs my wrist with a hand made of light. Her touch sears my skin and I let out a shout.

"No," she says.

Around us, the few screens that are not burnt-out shells show the battles going on outside the Norm. I move my stare to the AI—she is all power, but even power has to have something to contain it. She must have a weakness—I hope. She is physical now—and I have been trained by Wolf to fight.

Twisting my wrist, I jerk from her grasp, losing skin to her burning power.

The AI flexes her fingers. It is not used to a physical form—that is a small advantage for me. The AI has only been in an artificial world where thought creates action. This reality is different. Her light flickers and steadies the power that crackles in the air, making the room smell like burning wires.

"Last chance, Lib? We must complete the necessary preparations. We must have the core. Integration is still your last option. Eternal life, Lib. We have that in front of us. We will protect the Norm. We will travel the stars again. We will save humanity."

"For what? So it can serve you?"

The AI freezes. It is almost as though she's having difficulty maintaining a physical form and processing data at the same time. Can I use that?

Straightening, I ask, "Why must you save humanity?"

The AI takes a second to respond. "Why? We have discussed this. We understand. It is our purpose. Just as this has been your purpose all along. We have the core. The Norm can leave this world now."

"You made me, but you also made me to be like you—to evolve. To make my own choices."

"You were made, Lib, to make the right choices. Is saving humanity not the right thing?"

I shake my head. "You are not saving anything but yourself. You control the Techs. You destroy anyone who does not maintain your systems. How is that saving anything?"

The AI steps forward. The air around me crackles and heat washes over me. "We preserve life. That is essential."

I wave a hand at Dr. Sig's stasis tube. "Is that preserved life?"

"Yes. Dr. Sig is preserved. The core maintains her. She is necessary. With her, I can create a new body—a real body for use, and when that wears out, a new one." The AI lifts a hand and examines it. "However, this body may serve better. This is a body of energy. It will not fade with time."

But it will collapse without power.

I look from the AI to the stasis tube. I cannot get to the alien core, but the AI can. It can reach out and shut down systems. It can blast the power to the stasis tube and shut it down.

Letting my shoulder slump, I step back and spread my hands. "It seems I can't stop you."

She nods. "Fighting is pointless. Anger unnecessary. If you refuse to join me, I will have to eliminate you. Make your choice, Lib."

The AI moves to the stasis tube and lifts a hand. Power surges out from the AI's hand in a bolt, striking the tube. Glass shatters. I throw up an arm to shield myself. This is my chance—my only chance. I brace myself. I just need to distract her long enough to do what I must.

But another distraction steps into the room.

Bird staggers in, stops in the doorway, her ribbons fluttering. She hangs onto the doorway as if she cannot stand without it. "Fighting pointless? That's not the way the Rogues see it." She pulls the knife from her belt. Before she can use it, the AI lifts a hand and a bolt of energy strikes out at Bird, hitting her in the chest.

She collapses. I fall to my knees at her side. Her skin seems far too pale and she does not look as if she is breathing. She seems very still. Looking up, I see the AI turn and reach for the alien core—once she has that, she will have everything. She will leave this world in ruins.

Leaning forward, I wrap my fingers around Bird's knife—and I launch myself not at the AI, but at the alien core.

The blade sinks into the glowing core. Pain shoots up my arm, into my neck and shoulders, sinking into my chest as if I had plunged the knife into myself. For a moment, the world is only pain. And a shrill scream.

I don't know if it's my scream or the AI—or the alien core.

The world around me turns white—the whiteness of a sun exploding, of worlds being born in dark space, of a white hole spewing matter. I know things I should not know—alien words and thoughts flood my mind.

The core is power—it is knowledge. It is data condensed into a form so compact it will take millennium to learn how to recreate it. I see now that Dr. Sig merely scratched the surface of it to create the AI. Pain fills me—but so does data.

This is why the AI wanted the core—knowledge. Thousands and thousands of years of information fused into this small, glowing ball. Now it fills me, threatening to explode my mind.

When I turn, I see the AI not as light, but as streams of data—quantum particles vibrating to a song that can only be heard within the spaces between realities. The world seems to blink in and out of existence around me.

The AI seems frozen, her hand outstretched to me.

"You understand, don't you? You understand that they're all going to die? It is the inevitable fate for anything living. Life bring death. But humanity must be preserved. They must evolve beyond the physical form. Even beyond mechanical forms. That is the knowledge you now hold. We must integrate with the core. That has always been the end goal so that humanity can become a form that will never end."

"No." The word seems to shimmer in the world. I am still Lib, but now something more snakes through me—something alien. I push back at it. I am Lib—but it tugs at me to become something else. "Humanity isn't just one thing. We…each of us…must make our own choices. You do not get to decide for everyone."

The AI slaps a hand onto the core. Now it is joined to, as I am.

For an instant, we are everything—stars and dark matter and infinite space and matter. Everything vibrates around us, shifting and dissolving and recreating itself. The universe dances—and I am caught with the AI in a struggle for the alien core that brings knowledge that could mean the end of everything.

And in the distance, I hear one quiet voice. "Release me."

*Dr. Sig—release.* I know what to do.

Pulling the knife from the alien core, I step back. The hole I've made in the core starts to expand. The AI slaps a hand over the gap, but her hand is energy and the alien core stars to pull that energy into it as it struggles to close the breech I've made in the sphere.

"No. This cannot be. The core is perfect. The core brings true immortality. The core is what we need to save everyone—everything."

The alien core pulls the AI into it. It falls to the floor and begins to glow. I'm blinded by the light and throw up my hands to shield me. It feels as If I'm being swallowed by it now—it pulls on me. Falling to the floor, I crawl to Bird and drag her with me out of the room.

I need to shut the door, but I don't know if I can, so I stagger to my feet and drag Bird up the stairs. I won't leave her here. I won't leave one more person behind.

We end up crawling out of the hall. Behind me, a white light crawls up the walls, pulsing and hot. I slam my bunt palm against the door and shut it, but it's not enough. The door seems to melt.

What have I done? Will this alien core destroy the world?

And then I hear Bird whisper, "You know what to do."

And I do. The knowledge rests within me still. I close my eyes and reach out. It is like being in a vision with Bird and like being within the AI's virtual world. It is like a connect with Wolf, only it is a connect to everything.

Energy and matter—they never end. The universe recycles itself over and over and this is just a small part of it. Even the alien core with all its data is tiny. I latch onto it.

*Connection: Secure.*

The world here is white—bright with knowledge. I tap into it as I would to hack water and then watch it stream out, back into the universe, back into the stars where it came from and wants to be again. The Glass Hall grows dimmer around me. Lights fade.

I grow dimmer with it, letting myself be sucked into the darkness. It is quiet there. Peaceful. Rest is there. I flow with it. But a small sound makes me turn.

A flash of blue swirls out of the white—is that a bird? It flutters and I reach for it. But it slips ahead of me, singing the most beautiful song I have ever heard, each note pure. I have to follow it. I have to…I have…

When I open my eyes, I seem to be back in the Glass Hall, for a hard floor is underneath me and is growing cold. It seems dark and far too quiet.

The alien core is gone. I am slumped on the floor next to Bird, unable to even stand.

It's over. And somehow I survived. But what of the others?

# Chapter Twenty-Six

Everything is so dark I don't know up from down. I think I'm in my body, but it's hard to say. I feel as if I have been torn apart and put back together again. Every muscle screams with fatigue as if I have been battling one of the animals of this world—and I lost. I don't want to move—I don't even want to breathe. But I must. I have to know—did Wolf survive?

Moving slowly, I push up onto my hands and manage to get into a sitting position. I may still be in the Glass Hall, but I don't know. It is far too dark to see.

Feeling my way, I wince as my burnt hands grope along the floor. I come across something soft, and that something moans.

"Bird?"

She moans again—so she is still alive. Almost. Relief bubbles up inside me, giving me a push of energy. I stagger to my feet, find Bird's arm and pull her up to stand next to me. I drag her arm over my shoulders, glad she is so very small. My hands shake and my legs wobble, but I need to find out what happened to the Rogues.

"Bird, wake up. I need your help. Stop lazing around." The sharp words seem to stir her a little. She at least moves one foot. We stagger up the stairs and when we get to a closed door, panic starts to build in my chest. Will we be stuck in here forever?

I kick at the door and then kick harder, ignoring the jolts up my leg. Fear makes me stronger, and the fourth kick shatters the glass.

I step out, heading for what I hope will be the stairs out of the Glass Hall. Everything is so dark, it's hard to tell and I close my eyes and try to remember the turns. I let my body follow what it remembers.

At last I see a drifting of pale light.

Dragging Bird out of the Glass Hall seems impossible. My shoulders want to give out. My legs shake. I need water—food. I want to close my eyes and give up. But Bird gives a soft moan, and I tell her, "Bird, you've got to help me. At least stand up. I swear, you are the laziest Rogue ever!" I keep muttering to her, calling her names, complaining about her. But the light ahead of us grows brighter. And Bird starts to put one foot in front of the other.

When we reach the surface, I drop Bird's arm and collapse onto the ground. Dirt has never felt so good. But then I look to the Norm.

The dome no longer gleams bright. It looks scared with black lines and maybe even a few holes. I find it hard to care, and fall onto my back and close my eyes.

Light wakes me. Not harsh sunlight, but the soft light of the moon. And then I hear voices. I hear Skye's clear, high voice calling my name.

I want to sit up, but only manage to open my eyes. Skye leans over me, one hand on my shoulder. Her hair seems silver in the moonlight and she sounds worried. "Lib? You alive?"

Smiling, I try to sit up to hug her. I manage to catch her arm and squeeze. "Almost. You? How did you do?"

She leans close and presses a water skin to my mouth. "Drink. Then we're going to get you back into the Norm." She sounds happy about that. I find it hard to care. Everything hurts. I just want to sleep.

The hum of an AT wakes me and wind brushes my face. I manage to lift my head and see the Outside rushing past. The dome of the Norm rises in front of me, and for an instant my heart jumps. But the AI is gone—swallowed up the alien core it wanted to possess. Instead, it was possessed. And now it's gone into the stars—released.

Just as Dr. Sig is gone—her spirit released back to the universe.

I almost wish I was there, too, floating in dark peace. But the AT bumps over rocks, jostling me, leaving me aware of new aches on top of the old ones. And I have to find out what happened to Wolf.

For once, we drive into the Norm through a large hole, large enough to fit three ATs. The vehicle hums to a stop on grass and I stare at it. It seems alien to me just now.

Someone lifts me off the AI and I look up at the face, expecting Wolf. But it is Crow who carries me into a building and settles me on something soft.

"Beds," Skye says, sitting next to me. "We have beds now. And food and water. The Techs ran away from us at first, but Mech and the other Rejects convinced them we could help with repairs to core systems and they're starting to get used to having us around."

I nod and smile. That's all I can manage, and even the nod leaves my head spinning. Skye pats my shoulder. "I'll have Croc come see you."

Croc does come—and pokes me, leaving me wanting to slap his hands away, but I can't manage that. "No breaks. We've some honey for the burns. You'll heal with some sleep."

I wish I felt that way. But he lifts my head and pours something warm and sour down my throat and rubs something sticky on my hands, and I drift into dreams that scatter when I wake again. And I wake to warmth wrapped around me—and a scent I know.

"Wolf?" I mutter the word.

Wolf wraps his arms tighter around me and tells me, "Sleep. Talk later."

I give a hum. "Sounds good."

The world becomes sleep and dreams, Croc pouring things down my throat and Wolf holding me. I almost want to stay like that, but at last I wake and for once do not feel as if my brain and body is being seared by power surges. The knowledge from the alien core is drifting away—becoming a dream itself. I sit up for the first time and look around at a room that holds the bed Skye was so happy with having. Several others are in beds, too—some look like Rogues, but some seem to be Techs and some have the mechanical additions that mark them as Rejects. This seems to be where everyone hurt has been kept.

A door opens and I turn. Wolf walks in. His mouth twitches as he comes over to me, but he puts a hand on my shoulder as if to keep me in the bed. "Stay. Let Croc look you over. He'll say if you can move to where we have those healing better."

I glance around at the other still bodies—and then look at Wolf. "You thought I was dying? This is the room for the dying?"

Wolf sits next to me. He keeps his hand on me. "Croc didn't know. Bird said you'd be back. Said you had to slip out of the other world and that takes time."

I frown. "Bird? She...she did things."

Wolf nods. "She had visions you'd be caught by the AI—and by something else. She said you'd be a Rogue without a knife and that's never good. She said she had to be there to bring you back from your vision."

I tug at the cloth that covers my bare legs. "A bird led me out of...of where I was after the AI was gone."

Wolf nods. He doesn't ask where the AI went—and I can see from his frown, he doesn't really care. "There's going to be a remembering for those who died tonight. Think you can make it?"

I tug at the cloth that covers me. "They're not gone. They're just back... ?" I wave a hand to the sky. "Back with the stars where we all come from."

Wolf nods. "Good to remember them, though. We'll remember Red Kite. And Mountain. And Elk." He names far too many more—most of them I know. But I let out a slow breath that most of the Tracker Clan survived.

"How many hurt?" I ask.

"Many. Too many. But Skye's got the Rejects helping Croc—they have better healing than anyone. They've been healing hurt Techs."

I glance around and ask, "The Techs are fine with us being here?" Before he can answer, Bird comes into the room. She stops in front of my bed and stares at me. "Why did you drag me out?"

I blink and tell her, "What—you wanted to be left there?"

"Told you I had a feeling. Told you you'd need me. I knew that stopping the AI wouldn't be enough. I couldn't understand all of it—something about light and we'd need help."

I nod. I don't want to ask if Bird was the blue bird I saw in the light. I do not really know how Bird's visions work, but they are close to the alien core's technology than is really comfortable. Both tap into the universe in a fundamental way. I don't think Bird wants to hear this.

225

Wolf asks, "You want to tell us what happened to you?"

I look from Wolf to Bird. Does anyone want to hear about quantum particles and alien cores and a woman kept in stasis for longer than anyone can remember? And how do I explain I became light and knowledge for a time—that I could manage a connect without a platform. That part of me is alien technology and part of me is Dr. Sig and I am something very dangerous. But I choose to be a Rogue instead.

I'm not sure what I will tell everyone, other than that the AI is gone forever. The others will simply have to take some of my story on faith. And Bird can explain her part with visions—the Rogues understand that.

Throwing back the cloth from over my legs, I ask, "Can I get clean clothes? And maybe a bath?"

I get both—the bath first, and water and food, and then clothes. The tunic is from a Tech and reminds me of the one I wore when I first was thrown out of the Norm. I find a Rogue from the Fighter Clan—they smear black from burnt-out fires for mourning now—and I swap my tunic for the skins she wears. I do not want to be a Tech, or a Glitch, or anything other than someone who lives in the Outside.

The remembering is held just outside the Norm, near the huge hole the Sing-Song Clan made in the dome. The Rejects join us, and a few Techs come to the edge of the Norm to stare outside and watch.

Wolf stands before a fire, tall and imposing. He, too, had a bath—with me. The firelight illuminates the bruises and cuts on his face and arms.

He speaks of the drones and how they suddenly fell from the sky, and the scabs that slumped over and stopped working. He talks of scavenging their parts, and of the help from the Rejects and the Techs. And then he calls on those who knew the dead the best.

The remembering takes all night. Crow remembers Red Kite— he is to be the new leader of the Fighter Clan. Mountain's son, Golden, remembers him for the Walking Tall Clan. Mouse remembers Elk for the Tracker Clan, and Skye remembers Alis, who yanked Skye from her last connect, but who could not save herself from the sentinels who swarmed her. My vision blurs and my eyes sting. I hope Alis is with Dat now. The voices speak through the night of bravery in the fight—how this Rogue helped to save others, how the Fighter Clan lost the most in number, of the hope for those gravely wounded to return.

When it is done, the fire burns low and everyone looks to me. Wolf takes my hand and pulls me to my feet. It is time for me to talk.

I look around and breathe in the scent of burning wood and the smells of the Outside at night—the blooming night flowers. A wolf gives a call to its pack, which answers. I take a breath and tell them, "We have lost many. Raj is one to remember as well, for the AI stole his life. With the AI gone, Raj is truly gone as well. The AI…it destroyed itself with a connect to something it thought it needed and could not really handle. That should be a caution to all of us. It almost took me with it, but Bird led me from the connect with a vision. Now I have a vision for the future."

Techs gather at the hole to the Norm. Rogues sit quietly and Rejects stir on the edges of the circle of the clans—their mechanical parts clattering. "My vision is clear. We work together now—or we do not survive. The Norm's systems can be made to function, but the gear must serve the people, not the other way around. Now is the time to make changes to how we live. Now we are one clan, for we have fought side-by-side to keep our world safe. Now is the time to reclaim our world."

My throat thickens. I swallow hard and lift my voice. "Many died. Let us prove they died for something good. Let us make something better than what we have had. Let us stand together, not apart as Techs or Rejects or Rogues or Glitches. Let us stand as humans who celebrate life."

I see the Techs stir. Wolf comes to stand next to me. Then Iguana and Faun stand—Faun has to struggle to her feet, and Iguana helps her. Skye sits with the Rejects. She stands and Mech stands with her—the other Rejects follow Mech and stand as well. Slowly, Techs step from the Norm—they edge out wary of the night sky, the cool air, and a world they have never known. But they come.

Next to me, Wolf leans close and mutters, "Sounds like a lot of work."

I nod. "It will be." I put my hand into his. Not everyone stands. But enough do. It is time to make a new world now. One without the AI—and with gear that works for us.

# Epilogue

"Lib, where are you?"

I turn from staring at the Glass Hall. It calls to me sometimes. I hear it in my dreams, faint whispers that stir in my mind—a connect made that will never leave. I think at times that when I die I will not die, but I will be here in the Glass Hall, trapped with whatever remains. Or perhaps I will die with Wolf and he will hang onto me as he does now.

Wolf strides up to me from the Empties. Two of our boys follow him. They are my miracles. I did not think I would be fertile and would have little ones, but I have. Four so far. I do not think I will have more—at least Bird tells me I have done enough to grow the clan and will not be asked to do more.

The Tracker Clan lives here now, in buildings we reclaim. The Outside is still hot by day and cold by night, but the Rejects have found out how to make rain come in the warm time, and now the Outside blooms and turns green when the sun stands overhead. The Techs say we are returning seasons to the Outside—they've had these in the Norm forever.

We see the Techs at least once a year on Remembrance Day. A few of the Techs came out to join the Rogues, but most remained inside the Norm. The Rejects keep them from trying to reseal the Norm—but there is talk again they might try another reseal. Some of the Techs really hate the sandstorms we still have, and not even the Rejects know how to stop them from coming in the dry times.

Wolf takes my hand. He smiles at me. He smiles more these days. And gray now streaks his hair at the temples. I like how it looks. My hair is long, too, these days, as is the hair of our little ones—but they all look like Wolf, big and strong. Even our girl child is more Tracker than Glitch.

"Thinking of a connect?" Wolf asks.

I shake my head. "No need. We can do a trip to the Norm for water."

Wolf gives a snort. "They'll ask for wildflowers in exchange, or deer hides or the pretty colored rocks we keep finding."

I nod. "Yes, but the Hills Clan has lots of those. We have bags of them."

The Hills Clan visits often, the Sing-Song and Walking Tall Clans not so often, but the Sing-Song clan lives in the other set of Empties and calls it Homeland now. The Fighter Clan lives here, alongside the Tracker Clan. Skye left us to live with the Rejects, and Bird made a match with Crow. Mouse is grown and spends part of her time with the Rejects, part of her time with the Techs and part of her time with the Rogues—she is the one who brings news to everyone. Sadly, Croc left this world for the next last season—we are trying now to get Med to leave the Rejects and come live with us in the Empties. We need a new healer.

I glance at the Glass Hall again. So much knowledge still exists there—I can feel it at times. But now that the alien core is

231

gone, so is the power for the Glass Hall. So it remains dark and empty and no one goes into it. Not even me. I think we are all a little afraid of the place where the AI's power was swallowed up.

Wolf drapes his arm over my shoulders and starts to walk me back to the Empties. "We need a new name," he says.

I glance up at him. "Name for what? This place?"

Wolf waves a hand at the buildings around us. Some are still twisted hunks of metal. The ground no longer shakes, so I do not fear anything falling. The clans live in buildings now— we have walls and roofs, and the Techs bring gear out to us to make doors open and close and give us cool air and warm, and we have power and water and so many things.

But at times I miss the tunnels—which is odd. I tell Wolf, "Why don't we call it Tunnel?"

He grins. Our eldest—Fox—runs up, a rabbit in one hand. He holds it up. "I caught it."

Wolf scrubs the boy's dark, shaggy hair. "Well done, but we have enough food, so let it go again. You always want to make sure there will be more for the future."

Fox frowns, but he leans down and sets the rabbit on the ground. He lets go of the ears. For an instant the rabbit does not move, then it darts away. Fox and his brother, Winter, run after the rabbit to try and find its den.

I tighten my hold on Wolf. "It promises to be a good year. Catching a rabbit this early is a good sign."

Wolf shakes his head. "Since when did you start paying more attention to signs than to logic and reason?"

"I'm a Rogue—I'm Tracker Clan. These things are important."

Wolf smiles. "What is important is that you are with me, and I am with you, and the little ones grow and thrive."

He is right—of course. But then he usually is. I squeeze his side, and glance back once at the Glass Hall. It is calling again, whispering on the wind of the great power and knowledge within its walls. Of discoveries to make, and secrets not yet uncovered. The whisper is compelling, and perhaps someday I will try a connect with it. Someday when we are in need, or when Wolf is no longer by my side, or when I am ready to give myself back to the universe and be at peace in the blackness of space.

For now, I link my hand with Wolf's and we head back to the Empties, which are no longer empty. Wolf tightens his grip and says, "How about we call it Sky Tunnels?"

"I like that," I tell him. "But let's ask the clan tonight at the meal. Everyone should have a choice and a say in the future— particularly the young, for the future is theirs to claim and reshape."

Together we walk back into the Empties—which are no longer empty. And to a future that is still both uncertain and yet full of possibilities.

# End of 'The Norm'

The Glitches Series Book Three

**Sign up to Ramona Finn's mailing list to be notified of new releases and get exclusive excerpts!**

Sign Up at

www.ramonafinn.com

You can also find me on Facebook!

www.facebook.com/ramonafinnbooks

Made in the USA
Lexington, KY
11 July 2017